GW01395894

Greenhill

by

Gary Cann

This story is a work of fiction.
Names, characters and incidents are the
product of the author's imagination or are
used fictitiously. Any resemblance to actual
events or persons, living or dead, is
coincidental.

Text copyright © 2013 Gary Cann

PROLOGUE

He woke and screamed. White again, nothing but white. He couldn't escape from the brightness, couldn't close his eyes, couldn't move even to turn his head. The scream was deafening in his ears, as it always was, but soundless in the air around him. No sound had come from his lips since he'd entered this place, wherever it was and whenever that was, no sound at all to disturb the room's oppressive silence.

And the white, the awful, bright, white. He couldn't shut it out and there was nothing to relieve it, nothing to break the monotonous lack of colour, at least as far as he could tell from the edge of his vision. He was naked, he knew that, but only from the lack of the feel of clothing or bed linen, but wasn't cold. Just naked and vulnerable and impotent to do anything about it or to protect himself.

He didn't know how long he'd been on this bed staring at a white ceiling, had no reference for time, no day or night, no minutes or hours. He didn't know what this place was or where it was. Come to that he didn't even know who he was, not anymore, had no memories to call on, no images in his mind but this white room. It was all he knew, unrelenting white. He screamed again. Soundlessly.

CHAPTER ONE

Malcolm Gregson felt guilty. Deeply guilty. Lost in thought, sitting in a patch of sunlight in the main hall of the crematorium, he was alone apart from a coffin and a bored looking undertaker. There were no other mourners, no friends and no family. The coffin lay on the crematorium bier, awaiting its short final journey, its occupant Amanda, Gregson's wife of fifteen years, who'd recently died after a short illness. She'd not been a well-loved woman, even by Gregson himself after a few brief happy years of marriage, and any friends and family had long since been driven away. Gregson had asked for a few minutes alone with his thoughts and the undertaker had obligingly stayed respectfully in the background. There was no vicar, no eulogy; there was no point. There was no one to hear it and Gregson knew all he wanted to know about his deceased wife.

It was time. He turned his head and nodded to the undertaker, who, waiting for the signal, walked slowly forward until at the front of the room he stopped by a lectern and pushed the button that was to start the coffin on its final journey. Gregson sat and watched as the hidden machinery burst almost silently into motion and stayed still in his seat until the curtains had closed behind the coffin. His sense of guilt surged at the sense of relief he felt as he shook hands with the undertaker and left the building.

Three hours later after a long quiet walk in the park, Gregson found himself in the pub a short distance from his home. He didn't want to go back to the house just yet. He'd not ever envisaged himself as a widower, but he had wondered, almost fantasised on many occasions about what life might be like if he'd not been trapped in a loveless marriage. But the whole widower thing was something he'd never thought about, well, not until his wife became seriously ill. Then the prospect had become a reality. But he still couldn't feel any emotion apart from the ridiculous guilt of not being upset.

It was noisy as he stood at the bar of 'The Bomb.' The place, which he'd rarely been in, was actually called 'The Bombardier's Arms', but this was too much of a mouthful for the regulars. These were, at the moment, restricted to a small group of elderly pensioners being crowded into a corner by an increasing number of young people.

"Bloody kids. They've no respect for anyone!"

"Drink themselves silly on that fizzy alcopop stuff. Got no sense."

"And always fighting when they've had a few. Either that or they're throwing up in the gutter. What's the point?" These and other similar comments were being bandied about by the older generation, while the youngsters simply got on with enjoying themselves.

Gregson wasn't a drinker; a coffee, preferably a latte, was more his style, but today wasn't a normal day. He ordered a whiskey and a half pint of bitter shandy and drank the spirits in one gulp while the shandy was being poured. Then, glass in hand, he weaved his way through to an isolated table, suppressing a cough from the whiskey. Sitting down to be alone with his thoughts, he drifted off into a semi-conscious reverie, his hand still around the glass.

His mind was following the same train of thought it had been since the day of Amanda's death and it was this that had him feeling so guilty. He was glad – no, that wasn't the word – he was relieved she'd gone. Now he had the rest of his life to live as he saw fit. She'd ruled the roost in their marriage and had taken advantage of his dislike of confrontation and arguments, and for his part, he'd settled for what he thought would be the easy life. Why had he never left? It was a question he'd often asked himself. Didn't have the courage to do it was the only answer he'd ever come up with, or as Amanda would have put it, he just didn't have the balls. A slap on the cheek roused him from his thoughts. A very hard slap, delivered with real feeling, which left his cheek stinging.

"You dirty git! What the hell do you think you're looking at?" A young woman, slightly the worse for wear from drink, had sat down opposite him while he'd been lost in thought. He was certain that she'd not been there earlier. The table had been empty. But what on earth was she talking about? And why the slap? It didn't take him long to work out what had made her so furious. She was wearing an extremely low cut blouse which left little to the imagination and she'd sat down right in his line of sight. He blushed, an experience he wasn't used to and stammering an apology, tried to explain that although he might have been facing in that direction, he wasn't actually looking at her or her body.

Or at least he was going to try very hard to explain. To explain that he'd been to his wife's funeral that morning and his mind was elsewhere, but he suddenly became acutely aware that people were staring at him and listening to him. Immediately uncomfortable, he stood up quickly making excuses about leaving. Doing so, he knocked over his still untouched glass of shandy, watching in horror as the contents rapidly flowed across the table and directly into her lap. He groaned as she leaped in the air, shouting.

"You stupid sod!" she screamed in a shrill drunken voice that made him wince. "Clumsy git! Look what you've done to my clothes!" The one thing Gregson didn't want to do was look. The girl's now sodden skirt was as short as her blouse had been low-cut and it was clinging to her legs.

"I'll pay for the cleaning," he said quietly, trying to calm her. "I'll give you my address. Send me the bill."

"You're bloody right you will. This stuff ain't cheap." Gregson gave her his address, which she shoved unceremoniously into

7

her handbag and then he hurried out of the pub, people's laughter ringing in his ears.

He was still cringing about the incident two days later when he had a dentist's appointment. He didn't find dentist's waiting rooms to be the most interesting or lively of places. They were, as a rule, even quieter than doctor's waiting rooms, as most people seemed more nervous about seeing their dentist than their doctor. The receptionists talked too loudly as if they were trying to make up for the silence of the patients, a radio was on, but so quietly it was barely audible and the magazines were either mind-numbingly boring or two months out of date, but mostly both. On his last visit, he'd begun reading A Beano annual of all things, and really enjoying it.

He looked around at his fellow patients for something to do, but hopefully not too obviously. An elderly man was leaning forward in his seat, both hands clasping the ornate handle of a walking stick; a harassed looking young woman with a baby in a pushchair was busily trying to keep the little one occupied, while in the corner on the other side of the room, a woman with long wavy red hair was reading one of the out of date magazines. Rather hippie-ish looking, and possibly in her late thirties, she was wearing an ankle length skirt and open sandals. But it was her ankle, just visible beneath the hem of her skirt that caught his eye. All in all, it was a very nice ankle, well shaped with lovely smooth skin, and it was what was on it that interested him. It was a tattoo of a rose, with the thorny stalk twined around her ankle, with a partially open rose-bud rather than a flower in full bloom. It was fascinating and eye-catching. Then she was called in to see the dentist and a movement on the pavement outside the window caught his eye and his attention.

Wearing a black t-shirt, black jeans and with styled natural looking blonde hair, the woman looked gorgeous, but that wasn't what made him carry on watching her. She walked somewhat provocatively along the High Street, her head held high, tanned arms swinging at her sides and hips swinging with a natural feminine rhythm and there was an air of familiarity about her that confused him. Who was she? For the moment, he couldn't place her.

He jumped slightly as the alarm rang on the mobile phone that he should really have switched off. He did so as the oh-so-attractive, but oh-so-stern looking receptionist glared at him accusingly. A dental nurse rescued him.

"Mr. Gregson? Could you come this way please?" He rose quickly and followed her out of the waiting room and into a treatment room. The appointment passed off gently and painlessly, with only the foul taste of pink mouthwash as a souvenir. Any thought of the woman he'd seen had gone completely out of his mind.

Leaving the dentist, Gregson decided on a coffee before returning home to his empty house. As the place he lived wasn't yet blessed with the likes of Starbucks, Costa or other global coffee shops – that would have meant a trip into Peterborough – he had to settle for his local café. Waiting to order his drink, he was innocently standing by the counter when he felt a hand on his arm.

"Malcolm Gregson! It is you, isn't it?" said a female voice. He turned in the direction of the voice and found himself looking into the face of a stranger, a rather glamorous and attractive stranger, the woman of the black t-shirt he'd seen from the dentist's window. He nodded absently and must have looked as vague as he felt, or even more so, as this vision of loveliness in front of him continued. "You don't remember me, do you?" She didn't allow him to answer. "Sonia Westerley," she said solemnly. "We went to school together."

Gregson's mind suddenly kicked into gear, leaping back through the years and he dropped a handful of change on the floor instead of handing it over the counter to the assistant. As he crouched and fumbled for the coins, Gregson's memory worked quickly and mercilessly. Of course he remembered Sonia Westerley. She'd been easily the most attractive girl in the school, and every single boy would have remembered her. He'd had a crush on her. Unbidden, memories came back to him of being a stammering shy idiot in her presence, blushing freely every time she even said 'hello' to him. Maddeningly, he felt those same feelings invading his mind across the years.

"Can I help?" she said, crouching beside him, her perfume filling his nostrils.

10

"No, no, I can manage," he said. The closeness of her body was distracting him, and the smell of her perfume, if a little powerful for his taste, was intoxicating.

"Then at least let me buy you a coffee and we can have a chat." How could he refuse? They found a corner table and as Sonia sat down Gregson couldn't help but notice how her figure had improved with the passing years. He looked away quickly; staring vacantly at a woman had given him enough trouble already this week.

"Well, Malcolm, tell me what you've been up to," Sonia said cheerfully. Gregson quailed inwardly. How could he put into words that he felt he'd done nothing with his life? She noticed his hesitation and smiled. "Wife, children, job, you know, that sort of thing." Gregson smiled back.

"You go first. I'm sure your life's been more interesting than mine. You always had ambition."

"Oh, I had ambition, Malcolm. Bags of it. But a lot of good it did me. Every girl's dream, that's what I had." She took a sip of her coffee and a milky moustache appeared on her upper lip. Gregson was slightly disconcerted at how sensuous it was when she unconsciously licked it away with her tongue.

"You sound bitter, Sonia," he said warily. He was rewarded with a warm smile.

"Do I? I'm sorry. I don't mean to. It's just that having got what I wanted as a girl, I found it wasn't what I really wanted. But life's

11

like that, isn't it? No, I'm not bitter, but maybe I am a little disappointed." She looked down at her coffee and then back at Gregson with a radiant smile that reminded him of her as a schoolgirl. "But it's all behind me now, and that's where it's going to stay. I have a life to lead, and I'm going to enjoy it." It seemed that both of them were a little wary of discussing their lives. They chatted about this and that without learning anything more about each other before she said quietly that she had to visit 'the little girl's room.' He watched her as she crossed the café.

Some women, he thought, naturally walk in an arousing way. A swing of the hips, a gentle motion of the buttocks, and a rhythm to the step that is positively erotic. This was the case as Gregson watched Sonia Westerley heading for the toilet. Her stylish clothes clung to her, emphasising her curves and high-heeled shoes brought attention to her shapely legs without seeming to be difficult to walk on. There was no doubt that she was extremely attractive woman. And way out of your league pointed out an irritating little voice in his subconscious. But he was happy to be having a pleasant conversation and a coffee with a woman who could turn men's heads simply by walking across a room. It gave him an unusually warm glow. Then she was back at the table, with her hand over his, smiling.

"It's been really nice meeting up with you again, Malcolm. A breath of fresh air that I badly needed," she said, resuming her seat. Gregson sensed an opportunity, a point where a decision needed to be made, and to be made quickly.

"It's lovely to see you too, Sonia," he said, playing for a little time and enjoying the feel of her hand on his. He really wanted to see her again. "Would you like to meet for a meal?" he asked, blurting it out like some impetuous teenage boy. The words were out of his mouth before he thought about what he was saying.

"A meal? Yes, that would be rather nice, Malcolm." The pressure of her hand on his increased slightly. "Very nice." They finished their coffees while making arrangements. Gregson found his heart racing. He'd probably have been more relieved if she'd said 'no.' She was apparently staying at the Mill Hotel, overlooking the river, a place Gregson knew to be expensive, and they agreed to meet in the hotel restaurant.

"Would tomorrow be rushing things?" Sonia asked. "I'm not sure how long I'm staying in town." Tomorrow? Gregson couldn't believe what he was hearing.

"Yes," he said, then "No, I mean tomorrow will be fine." She was smiling at him as she leaned over the table and gave him a quick peck on the cheek. She stood to leave.

"Until tomorrow then, Malcolm." She pulled on her jacket and with little girly wave, left the café. He watched her go, hardly noticing a young woman with a red shoulder bag rise from her seat near the door and follow Sonia out into the street.

CHAPTER TWO

The hotel in which Sonia was staying was, Gregson knew, the most expensive in town, and this slightly intimidated and unnerved him. His had been a fairly mundane, middle of the road sort of life and eating out in expensive restaurants wasn't something he was at all accustomed to

or particularly comfortable with. To make things worse, he was about to be sharing this meal with a very desirable woman. He was nervous.

Always prone to flights of imagination, or more properly, little flights of fancy, Gregson had tried to consider how the evening might go. Knowing that it was a purely platonic meeting, his male mind would still not let go of the idea that it might develop into something more, and while at one level that certainly appealed, at another, it merely made him more nervous than he thought he could be at his age.

He was early and waiting gave him too much time to think. He mentally shook himself into a more alert state and walked into the hotel. Feeling even more intimidated as soon as he entered the foyer, he felt an indefinable air of money hanging around the place. He crossed to the area marked 'Reception' hoping he looked more confident than he felt.

"Can I help you, sir?" said the smartly dressed young man behind the counter whose name badge announced him as Tyler.

"Yes," said Gregson. "I have a table booked in the restaurant."

"Then if you'd like to go that way, sir," the young man said, pointing across the foyer to a doorway clearly marked 'Restaurant,' "I'm sure one of the restaurant staff will be pleased to help you." Feeling firmly but politely put in his place by young Tyler, and with his already shaken self-confidence now bruised a little as well, Gregson crossed the foyer as he'd been directed. His path into the restaurant itself was then blocked by another young man in a similar uniform to Tyler, also with a name badge which this time Gregson took no notice of.

"Can I help you, sir?" the young man said in an echo of the receptionist.

"I'm here to meet someone for dinner," Gregson said.

"And the name, sir?"

"Gregson. Malcolm Gregson, but..." The young man's eyes flicked down to a book on a small desk.

"There is no reservation in that name, sir."

"As I said, I'm here to meet somebody," Gregson said.

"And the reservation is in their name, sir?"

"Yes," said Gregson. There was a long pause while the young man looked at him.

"And that name is, sir?" the young man finally asked. Was that a touch of impatience Gregson heard?

"Westerley," he said firmly. The eyes stayed longer on the book this time.

"No, sir. Still nothing." Gregson was confused. Had Sonia forgotten to make the reservation or worse still, changed her mind and not told him? She had no way of contacting him, he realised, nor he of contacting her.

"Are you sure?" he asked.

"Oh, yes sir, quite sure. There is definitely no reservation in the name of Westerley in the restaurant this evening." Gregson hoped he was imagining the sense of triumph he thought he could hear in the young man's voice. He glanced around to see that Tyler on reception seemed to be watching the whole interchange with some interest. "You do have the correct name, sir?" Gregson could have kicked himself. Westerley was her childhood name, the name he'd known her by in school. He tried to remember. She must have told him her married name. Some sort of animal. Wolf? No, that wasn't it. Something less ferocious. Fox. That's what it was.

"No, forgive me. It'll be booked in her married name. Fox."

"Her married name, sir? Very well." There was a slight tone of both humour and disapproval in his voice. Gregson nodded. The young man looked at his book again, shaking his head. Was that a smile as well? "Still no reservation, sir. Is the lady a guest in the hotel?" Gregson nodded again, a strange feeling of disappointment creeping over him. He felt a little old to be stood up on a date. "Might I suggest you talk to Reception, sir? There may be a message." Gregson glanced across the foyer towards the reception area, where Tyler was still watching him.

"Good idea. Thank you." At Reception once more, Gregson found himself going through the same routine with the same result. There was no message, and if the increasingly smug Tyler was to be believed, Sonia was not booked into the hotel and never had been. He turned away from the desk, still feeling Tyler's eyes on him, and sat down in one of the comfortable armchairs near the entrance, wondering what to do. As he was settling himself in and thinking about getting a coffee, a young woman entered the foyer from the street walking past him to sit in one of the other chairs. She placed a red shoulder bag on the table in front of her and looked as if she was preparing for a long wait. An aroma of strong flowery perfume hung in the air where she'd passed him.

His thoughts returned to Sonia. He felt a fool, but still hoped that there'd been some mistake or that there was a logical reason for this strange situation. Why had she suggested this hotel if she wasn't staying here? For that matter, why had she said she was? Many times in his life, too many times, there had been cause for him to doubt himself, but on this occasion he was convinced he was in the right. It had meant too much for him to have possibly got it wrong. He'd thought of little else since yesterday. Then there was a light tap on his shoulder and he looked up into the face of a slightly apprehensive looking young woman, wearing a similar uniform to Tyler on Reception, her tied back in an unbecoming pony tail.

"Excuse me, Mr. Greenhill," she said quietly, "but this is for you." She handed him an envelope. "A lady said you'd be here at this time." She walked hurriedly away before he could say anything. He stood up as if to follow her, but she'd already disappeared through a 'Staff Only' door. Sitting down again and turning the envelope over and over in his hands, he thought there must have some mistake. For a start, his name wasn't Greenhill, although it did seem familiar. Did he know someone called Greenhill? If he did, it wouldn't come to mind. He was about to take it to Reception, saying there'd been a mistake, even at the risk of talking to Tyler, who was currently talking to someone on the telephone, when he actually looked at the envelope.

It bore the hotel crest, along with a single word, 'Malcolm', not 'Mr. Greenhill.' So it was for him. Still looking at it, he realised he was nervous about what the envelope's contents might be. But there was only one way to find out, so he ripped it open and extracted a sheet of the hotel's headed notepaper. As he did so, a room key fell into his lap. He picked it up – not surprisingly, it was for this hotel. The accompanying note said simply 'Come up and see me. A time for reflection', with no signature. He looked from the note to the key and back again, increasingly nervous, but with a generous helping of curiosity.

He didn't consider himself a risk taker and never had; a job in a council planning department didn't engender that in a person.

Going to find the room to which this key belonged seemed like a risk, especially as he'd already made himself known to Tyler on Reception, who he was convinced was still watching him, his earlier telephone call now complete. He was also worried about what he might find there, unsure if he was up to facing whatever might happen, if anything did of course. He settled back in his seat, now fingering the room key rather than the envelope. Room 23 the key fob had on it as he turned it over and over in his hand. Room 23.

Noticing Tyler occupied with a guest checking in, Gregson made a sudden decision, rose from his seat and walked purposefully towards the stairs, expecting at any moment that someone, either Tyler or the young man from the restaurant, would ask him where he was going. No one did, and he quickly climbed two short flights of stairs to the first floor landing, and then, more casually, two more to the second floor, where a sign indicated that he should turn left through a fire door to find rooms 20 to 26.

He found the room easily, and checking there was no one in the corridor, inserted the key and quickly let himself in, feeling rather furtive. The room was in darkness, but after a little fumbling, he found the switch on the wall and turned on the lights. It was deserted; clean, tidy and apparently waiting for its next occupant. A typically anonymous hotel room. Hoping that the person checking in downstairs wasn't going to be that next occupant, Gregson looked around anxiously and urgently, opening drawers and cupboards, not knowing what he was looking for. There had to be something there to be found; why else had he been given the note? That thought made him stop for a moment and sit on the edge of the bed.

He knew this was all out of character for him and the thought sobered him a little, helping him think a bit more sensibly. He was only supposed to be here to share a meal with an old school friend and now he was behaving like the hero of some TV drama. But there was the rub; he enjoyed mysteries and puzzles, even though he might not be very good at them.

What had the note said? 'Come up and see me.' Well that was straight forward enough. 'A time for reflection.' Reflection? Thought? No, more simple than that; mirrors. Was that what he should be looking at? His search turned into a success with the shaving mirror in the bathroom. There was a small piece of paper tucked in behind it, out of sight of the cleaner. He unfolded it and found a mobile phone number; one thing was for sure, and that was that now was not the time, nor the place, to ring it. He tucked it into his jacket pocket, checked to ensure the room still looked tidy despite his search, and reaching for the door handle, switched off the light. On opening the door, he was unexpectedly faced with Tyler from Reception standing in the corridor, about to unlock the door. Behind him stood a young police constable and an older man in a brown suit, with, Gregson noticed rather incongruously, black shoes. Tyler stood frozen, key in hand, as surprised as Gregson.

"That'll be all son," the older man said, placing his hand on the receptionist's shoulder. As Tyler turned away down the corridor, the older man spoke again. "Malcolm Gregson? My name is Detective Inspector Townshend and this is Constable Whale. I'd like a word with you, sir." He gestured back through the still open door. It wasn't a request, and Gregson had no option but to agree. Speechless and with a sinking feeling in his stomach that things were not going well, he turned and re-entered the room. He switched the lights back on and sat on the edge of the bed again. The constable remained in the hallway while the Detective Inspector seated himself in the room's only chair, making himself comfortable as if he expected to be there for quite some time.

CHAPTER THREE

"Shall we start by finding out what you were doing in this room, and how you happen to have a key, Mr. Gregson? After all, you're not a registered guest at the hotel, are you?" His voice was calm and almost soothing, similar to a vicar's, Gregson thought as he struggled for an answer that might seem plausible. He certainly couldn't deny having been in the room, nor having the key, as it was still in his hand. The detective seemed amused at Gregson's hesitation.

"I was given the key in the foyer downstairs," Gregson said. Even though it was the truth, it sounded lame as he said it.

"Given it," echoed the policeman, a trace of disbelief in his voice. "And who gave it to you?"

"A young woman, in the hotel's uniform," replied Gregson nervously, already feeling he was doing nothing to improve what was undoubtedly an awkward position. "I've never seen her before."

"Can you tell me anything else about her? Was she young? Old? What was the colour of her hair?"

"Young, her hair tied back. I didn't notice what colour it was."

"Did she have a name badge?"

"I didn't notice," admitted Gregson.

"And she just handed you the key?"

"Yes, in an envelope." Gregson, on a sudden impulse, said nothing about the note. After all, it was probably only important to him. "An envelope addressed to me, using my first name," he added, hoping it was helpful.

"And it was just the key?" the detective asked. Gregson nodded. There was a pause during which he found himself becoming more and more uncomfortable. He wasn't used to dealing with the police. It was a new experience for him to be questioned like this, especially as he'd been caught red-handed doing something wrong. "And did the young lady say anything as she gave you the envelope?"

"Yes, as a matter of fact, she did. She said 'Mr. Greenhill, this is for you.'"

"Mr. Greenhill? Why did she call you that?"

"I don't know, but the envelope said 'Malcolm.'"

"Do you have it?" DI Townshend held out his hand and Gregson gave him the empty envelope. "And the key, please." The policeman dropped them both into an evidence bag. "Now let me see if I've got this right, Mr. Gregson. A member of the hotel staff gives you a key to a room in their hotel, a hotel which you're not booked into, and that key is in an envelope addressed to you." Gregson nodded. "And then you decide to go to that room. Now why is that?" Gregson thought about this for a few moments, but the policeman hadn't finished. "This young woman, who is on the hotel staff, and whom you say you have never seen before and can't really describe, obviously knew who you were. Don't you agree?"

"It could have been a guess," said Gregson.

"I don't think so, Mr. Gregson," the policeman said quite coldly. "Were there other people in the foyer?"

"Yes."

"So she could have given this envelope, clearly marked 'Malcolm," and here he held it up, "to any other man there. Or asked Reception if there were any guests with the name of Malcolm. But no, somehow she managed to give it to you." Gregson could see the logic of this, but shrugged his shoulders and said nothing. He didn't know why, but it seemed suddenly important not to mention that the girl had been told by a lady that he would be there, as it could only be Sonia. There was another long pause. Increasingly, he was wishing he'd never set foot in this hotel room, but there was still the mobile phone number, obviously left for him.

"Why were you in the hotel in the first place, Mr. Gregson?"

"I was here to meet someone in the restaurant," Gregson replied, thankfully on slightly firmer ground.

"And yet, having been given a room key by a young woman you didn't know, you came up here instead?" It didn't seem the action of a reasonable man the way the detective put it.

"No, it wasn't like that," Gregson said defensively. He was now starting to wish he'd sat in the chair. The bed was proving a little uncomfortable.

"No? Then tell me what it was like, Mr. Gregson. This person you were meeting at the restaurant, for instance. Were they a hotel resident?"

"Yes," Gregson replied firmly, then shook his head. "No, they weren't, but she was supposed to be..." His voice trailed off with the sudden certainty that what he was about to say was going to make even less sense to the detective than what he'd already told him.

"How would it be if we started at the beginning, Mr. Gregson? People have said I'm a very good listener." Without mentioning any names, Gregson explained about the dinner date and how, mysteriously, the person he was meeting had not only not turned up, but wasn't even registered as a guest at the hotel. Disconcertingly, the detective's gaze never left Gregson's face as he listened.

"What was this person's name?" he asked after a pause which Gregson was beginning to realise was characteristic of him.

"Does it matter?" he asked.

"When you're a detective, everything matters, Mr. Gregson."

"Sonia Fox. Mrs. Sonia Fox," he replied, emphasising her marital status. DI Townshend appeared to take no notice of the emphasis.

"Well there you are, Mr. Gregson. It does matter. It matters a great deal." Gregson, not understanding, must have looked bemused. The detective, shifting around on the chair, which must have been every bit uncomfortable as the bed, continued. "The station received a call that someone was acting suspiciously in the hotel," he said, noting with amusement that Gregson looked embarrassed. "A uniformed officer was going to come alone – in fact he's outside the door now – but the reception desk also said that person was asking for a Mrs. Sonia Fox."

"So you already knew that?" Gregson asked. Townshend ignored him.

"Given the circumstances, I was asked to come along as well." Gregson was still a long way from understanding. Despite not really wanting to know the answer, he had to ask the obvious question.

"What circumstances?"

"Well, Mr. Gregson, What makes your enquiries about Mrs. Fox of interest is that at 6 o'clock this morning a body was found near the canal in very suspicious circumstances."

"Sonia?" Gregson interrupted. The detective shook his head, and carried on talking.

"The woman in question hasn't yet been identified, but all of the identification she was carrying proclaims her to be Mrs. Fox. However, that isn't who she is." Gregson felt he was moving further and further from understanding each time the policeman spoke. "We've been unable to contact Mrs. Fox, Mr. Gregson, and then out of the blue we get a report that someone in a local hotel is asking for her."

"Are you saying I'm a suspect for something?" The hotel room was beginning to feel uncomfortably hot and Gregson was feeling more than a little anxious with the turn of the conversation. The detective shook his head.

"Not at the moment, no. I'm hoping you might have some information about Mrs. Fox," He said. "When did you actually see her or speak to her last?" Gregson explained about their meeting in the coffee shop the previous day. "And when did you last see her before that? Did you see each other regularly?"

"Not regularly. The last time was about twenty years ago," Gregson said with a little smile.

"Was this an accidental meeting? Neither of you had been in contact with the other?"

"No, I hadn't seen or spoken to Sonia since our last day at school together when we were eighteen years old." The policeman made no comment, and seemed to be waiting for Gregson to finish. "I asked her if she would like to meet me for dinner…"

"You asked her? Not the other way around?"

"No. asked her. She told me she was staying at this hotel and she'd arrange a table. When I arrived they hadn't even heard of her." He saw the detective smile.

"And the some stranger gave you the key to this hotel room." It was a statement not a question. Gregson nodded. "And you came up to the room." Gregson nodded again. "Why?"

"I don't know. A rush of blood to the head?" There was another long pause, just long enough to again become uncomfortable.

"Did you find anything?" the policeman eventually asked.

"No," said Gregson, a little too quickly and horribly aware of the mobile phone number in his pocket.

"Well, Mr. Gregson," the detective began with an air of finality that made Gregson's stomach lurch, "that would appear to be all. If you could leave your address and a contact telephone number, with the constable outside, you can go. Thank you for your help, but please bear in mind that I may well need to talk to you again."

CHAPTER FOUR

A short taxi trip took a stunned and worried Gregson home and he closed his front door behind him with relief. Turning into the living room, he sat in the armchair in which he'd spent so many hours alone while caring for his sick wife, kicked off his shoes and gazed at the blank screen of his television set. For over an hour he sat thinking, his thoughts tumbling over each other incoherently while he tried to find answers to questions he wasn't sure of. Then he stood up, walked to the kitchen and made himself a cup of coffee.

Loosening his tie with a sigh he placed the coffee on the table, his mobile phone next to it. Then he slipped his jacket off and hung it on the back of the chair. Sitting down himself, he then had to fumble behind himself in his jacket to find the slip of paper from the hotel room, which he put next to his phone. Drinking his coffee he kept looking at the number as if it was going to tell him something. What had he gotten himself into? Yesterday, he'd bumped into an old school-friend, who'd now seemingly completely disappeared. He'd then broken into a hotel room – he couldn't call it anything else, even if he did have the key – where he'd been caught and as a result interviewed by the police. On top of that there was a dead body involved, someone who'd been carrying Sonia's ID. He leaned back in his chair, gazing at the ceiling, trying to focus his thoughts.

He was still behaving uncharacteristically, he knew that, but picking up his phone and dialling that number still seemed a step too far. It was obviously what somebody – presumably Sonia – wanted him to do, in the same way that she had wanted him to go into the hotel room. But should he get involved any further? Should he have given the phone number to the police? The only answer he could come up with to that last question was: yes of course he should have; but he hadn't. Why not? Somehow he knew it wouldn't have been the right thing to do. He also knew that by making that decision, he'd already taken a giant step towards involving himself further, his hand shaking slightly, he reached for his mobile phone and tapped in the number. He listened to the ringing, more than half hoping the call would be redirected to voicemail. His heart skipped a beat when a slightly distorted female voice answered. It skipped another beat when he heard her speak his name.

"Malcolm, thank God you've rung. I knew you would." It was Sonia Fox.

"How did you know it would be me?"

"You're the only person with this number," she replied.

"Oh." He paused. "Sonia, what's going on," he began, but she cut him short.

"There's no time for explanation's now, Malcolm. I need your help. Can you come to Canterbury and meet me?"

"Canterbury?"

"Please, Malcolm. Yes, or no?"

"Yes, but I've got a few questions, Sonia."

"Thank you. I'll see you at the Cathedral chapter house at eleven on Thursday. I'll explain everything then". The phone went dead as the call was disconnected at the other end. He leaned back in his chair, his mind in even more of a whirl one quick phone call in which he'd hoped everything would become clear, and he was know more deeply involved in a situation that he didn't understand. Why Canterbury? Why him? He needed another coffee and just the action of physically making the drink helped settle his thoughts a little.

Of course he was going to go to Canterbury, and of course he was going to help Sonia, reluctantly and with reservations, but he was going to help. Deep inside was a suppressed adventurer, a knight in shining armour awaiting his quest. Sonia was his damsel in distress. He almost laughed at the idea. Who was he kidding? He actually felt like a non swimmer standing at the edge of very, very deep water and knowing that his next move would be to jump. Very reluctant, a little anxious at the unknown and just a little bit excited. But he was still going to go, not knowing what help might be expected of him, and not knowing what help he might actually be able to give.

CHAPTER FIVE

Standing in the glass, concrete and steel nightmare that was the main concourse of St. Pancras station, surrounded by rushing, noisy and almost faceless people, Gregson thought for the umpteenth time in just the last hour how much he disliked big cities and London in particular then he reconsidered. Disliked wasn't the right word. He hated big cities. Life is loud. Places are loud and people are loud. Metropolitan life is just louder than anywhere else, a never ending stream of noise that constantly assaults the senses. He needed a coffee.

Strolling around, consciously trying not to get caught up in the hustle and bustle of the station despite the dark looks from those rushing past him, he found various coffee shops and fast food outlets, all crowded to bursting. Eventually he spotted somewhere he could order a coffee and actually sit down to drink it. He knew he had forty five minutes or so before his train was due to leave, so he pulled a book out from his bag and settled down to block out the surroundings if he could. He was almost immediately interrupted.

"Do you mind if I sit here? All of the other tables seem to be full". Looking up from his book, trying to hide his irritation, Gregson nodded and pulled his own tray a little closer to create more room on the table. It was an elderly woman, unusually wearing jeans, and carrying a red shoulder bag. She had very much a granny look about her, the sort of woman that would be at her happiest fussing over a houseful of noisy grandchildren. But what seemed odd about the friendly welcoming face was a pair of cold, bright and piercing blue eyes. Gregson gave her a smile as she sat down opposite him. A faint aroma of a vaguely familiar flowery perfume drifted across the table, but he couldn't place it – probably one his wife had worn at sometime. He'd never been good at perfumes. He returned to his book, hoping to resume his reading, but his new companion seemed to want to talk.

"Are you off somewhere interesting? I always find railway stations so very exciting. Don't you? Have done since I was a little girl. Daddy always used to say I should have been a boy". She laughed. "I'm off to Canterbury. Decided a couple of years ago I wanted to visit all of the cathedrals in England while I was still able to get about a bit. Haven't got very far yet, though. Where did you say you were going?" The garrulous old lady had hardly drawn breath, let alone allowed Gregson to reply. "It's my first time to Canterbury. It's supposed to be the most beautiful of all the cathedrals but my favourite is Salisbury," she said. Gregson finished his coffee and returned his book to his bag. Mean though it seemed, he was now determined to find a way to not be sitting with this woman on the train, making polite conversation for the whole journey. He excused himself and headed off further into the depths of the station in search of a toilet. When he finally made his way upstairs to his platform, the Canterbury train was in. He boarded and found himself a seat.

Canterbury, a place he'd never been to, was, he'd discovered, the most visited city in England after London and pilgrims had been travelling to the place since the sixth century when Augustine built an Abbey there. Because of that he was vaguely surprised that the train was relatively empty. It wasn't a place he knew much about. The presence of a Cathedral, Chaucer's 'Canterbury Tales' and the murder of Thomas a Becket was about the limit of his knowledge. He settled back into what was an unusually comfortable seat for a modern train, and the train began to ease out of the station. Thankfully, he thought, he'd managed to avoid the old woman from the café and hoped he would be able to further avoid her later when alighting from the train. He had no wish for a travelling companion.

"Thank you for choosing to travel on South Eastern High Speed Trains," announced a very well spoken voice as the train began to gather speed. Once out of London, it didn't seem to Gregson, despite the comfort of his seat, to be a very comfortable ride and he was quite happy that he didn't know quite how fast the train was going. The rail journey was terminating at Ashford International Station, another gleaming glass and steel building with no character, just like St. Pancras. Only a small stream of passengers disembarked from their high–tech modernistic train to find seats on a slower and more mundane, but incredibly British mode of transport, a double-decker bus. As Gregson emerged from the building he felt a small tug on his sleeve.

"Hello again," said a chirpy female voice. Recognising both the voice and the scent of her perfume, Gregson turned with a sinking heart to find the old lady from the St. Pancras coffee shop walking beside him, still clutching her inappropriate red shoulder bag and now also pulling a small suitcase on wheels. "I thought I might see you on the train, but here you are anyway. Wasn't it an exciting ride?" He sighed and immediately hoped she hadn't noticed. She hadn't, or at least gave no sign that she had. He smiled at her as she continued speaking. "Oh, I do so hate double-decker buses, don't you? All that swaying from side to side is no good for the nerves, and I find it so difficult to manage those steep stairs." Gregson, although agreeing with every word, latched onto the opportunity it presented and guiding the old lady to a seat downstairs, went upstairs after explaining he wanted a good view of the Kent countryside, feeling a strange mixture of guilt and justification at deserting her when all she seemed to want was someone to talk to. As he sat, swaying and rocking uncomfortably to the motion of the bus, and unable to concentrate on the passing countryside, pleasant though it was, he found himself trying to place the perfume the old lady was wearing. He was sure he recognised it from somewhere, but where?

CHAPTER SIX

The cathedral opened its gates to the visiting public at ten in the morning, and large queues of tourists and school parties were gathering well before that time, much to Gregson's dismay. He'd been out and about in the pretty city for some time, having left the hotel after an early breakfast, and although he'd enjoyed wandering through the old winding streets, his apprehension about the meeting with Sonia Fox was playing on his mind. The last thing he needed was large groups of noisy unenthusiastic children waiting to gain entrance to the cathedral precincts. He looked at the queues, then looked at his watch and sighed. He had plenty of time, so there was only one place to go, a coffee shop. There was one almost next to the cathedral gates where he could watch the progress of the queue, so he ordered a coffee and tried to interest himself in his book. His dismay at the queue grew alarmingly when he noticed the old lady from the previous day standing in it. She was the last person he needed around when he met Sonia.

His coffee was long finished by the time the queue had diminished to a trickle; he rose from his table and made his way out to the ticket booth. His thoughts became a little sidetracked as he parted with his entrance money. He wasn't a particularly religious man, but he felt there was something wrong in having to pay for admission to a place of worship. He knew all the arguments about how much they cost to run, but it still didn't feel right.

The cathedral close, although a large open space, was crowded. Visitors were standing around as if almost too awed to enter, and the school parties had been broken up into smaller much more manageable groups supervised by already harassed looking adults, but the sheer size of the building dwarfed them all. The majesty of it made him stop, like all the others, and like so many pilgrims throughout the centuries, and just stare for a few moments. Then he headed for the main entrance in the south porch and went inside.

If the outside of the cathedral had made him pause and stare, the interior simply astonished him. He'd never seen anything like it. Television and photographs didn't come anywhere near doing it justice. He felt his eyes drawn upwards following the line of the pillars and then up further and further to the roof which seemed so far away. Other visitors were doing the same. He felt a pang of disappointment at not having time to admire it or drink in the atmosphere, but not only did he have an appointment in the Chapter House, one of the volunteer visitor guides was descending on him with a determined look in her eye. He gestured at his visitor's map.

"I'm OK, thanks," he said. "Just going to have a wander around." She stopped in mid-advance and smiled.

"Please make sure you're careful on some of the steps. They're very worn," she said, and as she turned away in search of another victim, Gregson checked his map of the cathedral, then his watch, and set off for the Chapter House. The map directed him towards the Cloisters, passing what it told him was the actual site of Thomas a Becket's murder in 1170. Four knights, acting on what they thought were the king's instructions, profaned the sanctity of the Cathedral and hacked the archbishop to death in front of horrified monks.

The cathedral had effortlessly absorbed the huge number of visitors, while still retaining its air of tranquillity and calm, and even the school groups were hushed. The Cloisters, cool and airy in the warm sunshine, were surprisingly almost deserted, with just one elderly couple looking around and one young girl deeply engrossed in a book.

The entrance to the Chapter House was in the eastern passage of the Cloisters; he walked in through the open doorway and looked around. It was empty. No visitors had made it this far around the cathedral yet, nor, thankfully, had the guided tours, and he had the place to himself. Another check of his watch; he was early, but no matter. He sat down to wait, reading a little to pass the time, and discovering that Canterbury's Chapter House was the largest in England, and is impressive not only because of its size, but also because of the beauty of its ceiling, carved from Irish oak. Dutifully and almost automatically, he looked up, wondering at the same time how the monks could possibly have remained sitting on these uncomfortable seats for any length of time. After a few minutes of shuffling in an effort to get comfortable, he rose and walked around for a few minutes before returning reluctantly to his seat.

People came and went, some more quickly than others. School groups in particular seemed to spend more time in there, but still there was no sign of Sonia. Absorbed in his own thoughts, divided almost equally between a concern for what might have delayed Sonia and his own comfort, he was only vaguely aware of someone sitting down next to him.

"She's not coming, you know." He immediately recognised both the voice and the perfume.

"Sorry?" he said, turning to face the old lady from the train.

"I said she's not coming, Mr. Gregson." She sounded irritated at having to repeat herself, and the sickly sweet smile from the previous day was nowhere to be seen.

"How do you know my name?" he asked. "And who's not coming?"

"Don't play games, Mr. Gregson. There's too much at stake and to be honest with you, I haven't much patience." There was an edge of something in her voice which made him nervous. "Now, I want you to do as I tell you. We are going to get up and leave the cathedral together so we can have a quiet chat. And please don't do anything silly."

"For some reason, I don't think coming with you would be a good idea," he found himself saying, despite being conscious that he might very well be in danger.

"Don't be a fool. Do you actually think you have a choice?"

"Everyone has a choice," he said, playing for a little time as a group of tourists led by a cathedral guide appeared in the Chapter House doorway, stopping in a huddle to admire the room. Without warning, as the guide began her spiel about the ornate ceiling, Gregson bolted for the door, elbowing indignant people out of the way, and taking the old woman by surprise. Ignoring the complaints of the aggrieved tourists, he ran through the Cloisters and directly out of the exit into the cathedral close without going through the cathedral itself. Mingling with larger groups of visitors so as not to draw attention to himself, he watched anxiously for any sign of pursuit, feeling fairly confident that if she did appear, he could out-run the strange woman.

There was no sign of her as he moved closer to the exit which was through the gift shop, and he kept asking himself why he'd run. There had been something wrong with the situation, something that worried him and, he thought, something dangerous. But why? He'd only gone there to meet Sonia. He joined a group of pensioners moving in the direction of the shop and the toilets and as he peeled away from them into the shop entrance, leaving them to wander on up through the close, he noticed the woman standing by the south porch, talking into a mobile phone. She didn't seem to be bothering to look for him.

Once in the shop, he ducked behind a display stand containing ornaments at the sort of vastly inflated prices that only gift shops at tourist attractions seem to be able to get away with, and crouched as if looking at something on the bottom shelf. Then he glanced towards the shop exit, past the tills and into the street beyond. There seemed to be only crowds of tourists and shoppers, which was what he would have expected. The old woman hadn't yet come through the shop, so he didn't really know what he was looking for. Men rushing around waving guns? Sirens? Helicopters? He suddenly felt foolish and straightened up, smiling. This was Canterbury in England. Things like that didn't happen in places like this.

The shop was now his only way out, as there was no exit back into the cathedral close, not that he wanted to go that way. Slowly and calmly he walked out of the shop, smiling at the girl on the till as he passed her. Losing himself in the crowd outside, he relaxed a little, only then realising how tense he'd become.

He'd surprised himself by what he'd done and he took some satisfaction from thinking that if he'd surprised himself, then he'd most certainly surprised the woman in the Chapter House. But then the questions started to come. How did she know his name? He'd not told her in their brief meetings the previous day. Who was she? He'd no idea. How did she know he was meeting someone and that it was a woman he was meeting? Again, he didn't know. He'd not told her. But most worrying of all, particularly for Sonia, was how could she be so certain Sonia wasn't coming?

CHAPTER SEVEN

He was walking past a supermarket when his mobile phone rang, scaring him silly. He fumbled for it in his pocket, but just as he got his hand on it and pulled it out, it rang off. He looked at the number of the missed call. Damn! It was Sonia and he'd missed her. He pressed 'redial' only to hear the busy signal. With nothing for it but to wait for her to ring again, if she did, he kept on walking, without any idea of where he was going, and with frequent glances over his shoulder. A ping from the phone told him a text message had come in. From Sonia's number. 'Coffee shop Dane John Gardens' was all it said. He had no idea of where that was, so he either had to ask somebody or find an information board. Thankfully, he found one of the latter quite quickly.

Dane John Gardens turned out to be a public park only a few hundred yards from where he was standing. Idly curious about the strange name and suddenly nervous again, he read on, putting off the meeting by just a few more minutes while composing himself. The name was probably, he read, derived from the French word 'donjon,' the park being close to the castle, a building he hadn't even been aware that Canterbury possessed. Useless information given the situation, he thought, but interesting nonetheless.

Conscious that someone might still be following him even though he thought that if someone had been chasing him, they would have caught him by now if they'd really wanted to, he made his way down the road to Dane John Gardens. It turned out to be a very pleasant park, with tree lined paths, plenty of benches, the obligatory statues and a strange unmissable mound on one side, butting up against what remained of the ancient city walls and topped by a monument of some sort.

In the lee of the mound was an ornate bandstand and across the way from both was the coffee shop that turned out to be more of a kiosk with some unoccupied tables and chairs outside. Gregson bought himself a coffee and sat to wait for Sonia yet again. There were a fair number of people about, all of whom seemed intent on passing through the gardens as quickly as possible on their own business and none of whom paid him any attention. By the time he'd finished his coffee, there was still no sign of Sonia. He took his cup back to the kiosk and decided to take a look at the mound.

It looked like it could be a good vantage point over the park and coffee shop, so he decided to climb to the top, hoping that it wouldn't be too strenuous. A short walk took him past a deserted children's play area and to the base of a footpath which wound its way upwards in a spiral fashion. Unsure of whether or not he was doing the right thing as he'd still not spotted Sonia, he started up the mound. It didn't take long to reach the summit, which rose above the city walls and gave a good view of the busy ring road beyond. He sat on the seat running around the monument, watching the various paths through the park and waiting patiently once more for Sonia to put in an appearance.

"I'm so glad you took notice of the text message, Mr. Gregson." A man in a suit was standing over him, a smile on his face and a hand extended in greeting. He was very well spoken, with an air of authority, and Gregson instinctively took the hand, receiving a firm handshake.

"How do you know who I am?" he asked. The other man waved away the question as unimportant.

"I believe you've had a lucky escape," he said, taking a seat.

"Escape?" Gregson tried to sound vague.

"Don't be coy, Mr. Gregson. In the cathedral," the man said, smiling again. Gregson stayed quiet. "Have you any idea what you've got yourself involved in?" the man asked bluntly. It was the same question Gregson had been asking himself.

"Did you send that text message?" he asked instead.

"Yes."

"So you have Sonia's phone?"

"Yes." The man's smile was beginning to irritate.

"Where is she? Is she alright?" he asked.

"Ah, that I'm afraid I can't answer." The smile slipped a little. That wasn't what Gregson wanted to hear.

"So what's your interest in her, and what's your connection to the woman in the cathedral? She followed me all the way from London."

"Oh, she followed you further than that, right from your home, actually, but don't fool yourself, it's not you she's interested in, Mr. Gregson, and just for the record, neither am I really, rude as that may sound. A word of warning, by the way. That woman is dangerous." He paused to let his words sink in. "It's Mrs. Fox that everybody seems to want and it's in her interests if I find her first." The smile had completely disappeared now, although the man still seemed friendly enough.

"This all sounds very vague," Gregson said.

"I would imagine it does. Come, let me buy you a coffee and I'll explain what I can. And please, Mr. Gregson, trust me. There is no need to run this time." He stood and Gregson rose as well, but more slowly.

"And the woman in the cathedral?"

"When we have our coffee, Mr. Gregson, when we have our coffee." He was as good as his word. As soon as they descended to the coffee shop, had coffees and were seated again, he continued. "You asked about the woman in the cathedral?"

"Yes," said Gregson. "Who is she?"

"Who she might be is of no consequence, Mr. Gregson. What is important is that she and her team have been dealt with, at least temporarily."

"So there's no one following me at the moment?"

"Not that I know of, and believe me, I would know. I also think you're due an explanation of what's going on." Gregson took a sip of coffee, looking at the other man and taking in his appearance properly. He had a rather military bearing, greying hair and clear, intelligent hazel brown eyes, in a friendly, and at the moment, smiling, face. Gregson's impression was of what he would have described in his student days as a member of the establishment. He also looked, to Gregson's limited experience, a man to be trusted.

"So who are you, and how do you know me?" he asked.

"Blunt and to the point, but a good place to start, Mr. Gregson," the older man said. "Keith Blakeley is the name."

"And if it's not too impertinent, who is Keith Blakeley?" Gregson suddenly didn't feel in the mood to pussyfoot around. In the last couple of days, something seemed to have happened to his self confidence. Because he didn't know what was going on, it made him a little unsure, but the only was to brazen this through if he was to find out what was going on. As if to disarm him completely, Blakeley laughed.

"Detection and protection," he said.

"Is that some clever way of saying you're a private detective?" Blakeley laughed again.

"No. I suppose a better way of putting it is that I'm in the security business, Mr. Gregson."

"And the woman in the cathedral?"

"A rival business," was all that Blakeley would say.

"You're not giving me much of an explanation so far," Gregson said. "Does that make you as dangerous as you say she is?" Blakeley said nothing, merely took a sip of his coffee, pulling a face as he did so. His hazel eyes never left Gregson's face. "Are you going to tell me what I've found myself tangled up in?" Blakeley took another sip of his drink, then pushed it away.

"A number of people wish to find Sonia Fox, including Joseph Fox." Ah, her husband, Gregson thought, although Blakeley didn't say so. "Oh by the way, he's hired his own investigator who you may or may not meet at some point, but don't worry about him, he's all bluster. She appears to have something that we all want. What that is, from your point of view, is neither here nor there. She disappeared for a short period, but we, and by that I mean all of the interested parties, tracked her down to Peterborough of all places, where she met you, Mr. Gregson"

"Quite by accident, for a coffee," Gregson interrupted. "We were at school together." Blakeley gave him a look that said, in no uncertain terms, that he didn't believe anything in life happened by accident.

"Possibly," he said, seeming to confirm the look. "Possibly. But when she left you in the coffee shop, we lost her. All of us. A little careless perhaps, but there you have it. She knows what she's doing. All that we were left with was the knowledge that you were meeting her again."

"You knew that? How?"

"No matter. Call it a trade secret. The point is that you then became everyone's best hope of finding her, so we followed you." Blakeley looked as matter of fact as he sounded. Gregson drained the last of his coffee.

"To the hotel?" he asked. Blakeley nodded.

"Where Mrs. Fox seemed to have changed her mind about having dinner with you." Gregson looked at him in disbelief. The tables around the coffee shop were filling up as people emerged into the sunshine for their lunch breaks and it was becoming awkward for the two men to continue sitting without drinks, so ignoring his almost untouched coffee, Blakeley offered to fetch more drinks. Gregson knew he should simply get up and walk away, but the opportunity passed without him doing anything. As Blakeley sat down, Gregson decided to steer their conversation away from the hotel room and the police becoming involved. Blakeley probably already knew. He seemed to know everything else.

"So you followed me to Canterbury, still hoping I'd lead you to her?" As Blakeley nodded, Gregson continued. "How is it that you've got her phone and how did you know it would be me that you were ringing?" Blakeley took a sip from his fresh drink and smiled.

"Earl Grey. Not quite right when it's not served in bone china, but better than the coffee, believe me. As to your second question, simple guesswork. The only call received on that phone was two days ago, just hours after your missed dinner engagement. It just had to be you. As to how I happen to have the phone, well let's just say that sometimes things happen by luck, even for us professionals. It was found in the driveway of Mrs. Fox's home, here in Canterbury." The smile on his face was irritating, Gregson thought to himself again.

"She lives here?"

"Oh, yes. We've had her house under surveillance, but there must have been a cock-up of sorts, because she slipped in and out without us noticing. But she did drop her phone. Careless." He brandished it as if it were a trophy.

"What is it you want me to do?" Gregson asked, thinking how convenient and simple everything sounded. "And why is it you can't do it yourself? Why trust me?"

"If Mrs. Fox contacts you, we want to know about it. Nothing more. I think she may be in some sort of difficulty, even in some danger, and we can't help her if we can't talk to her." Gregson noticed he didn't get an answer to his other two questions.

"That simple?"

"Yes, and you know the number," he said, holding up the phone again. Gregson nodded and Blakeley stood up to leave, draining his cup of Earl Grey. "Please keep in touch, Mr. Gregson."

CHAPTER EIGHT

Left alone at the table, Gregson tried not to think. He didn't want to think, just wanted to clear his mind. There were still too many questions and not enough answers. He jumped as a newspaper was dropped on the table in front of him and looked up sharply.

"I did say I might want to talk to you again, Mr. Gregson, but I wasn't expecting it to be here in Canterbury," said a smooth velvety voice, "but you might want to read this article before we have a little chat." Detective Inspector Townshend seated himself in the chair vacated only a few minutes before by Keith Blakeley.

Gregson, surprised as he was by the presence of the policeman, was further surprised by the choice of newspaper even before he started reading the article. Not a national daily, as he might have expected, or a local Canterbury paper, but a Cambridgeshire paper. He looked at the headline of the article, 'Investigation as blaze destroys home,' and glanced up at the detective.

"Keep reading," said Townshend. Gregson did, reading aloud. The detective listened, even though he already knew what it said.

"A severe fire completely destroyed a local house in Milton Avenue yesterday afternoon." That was where he lived. "The Fire and Rescue Service were called at 12.20 pm, with three fire vehicles on the scene tackling the blaze. The occupier of the house is apparently away." Gregson looked at the photograph and then at the policeman. "You know that's my home, don't you?" Townshend nodded and Gregson carried on reading. "It took fire-fighters until early evening to put the fire out. The Fire Investigation Team attended the incident in an attempt to discover the cause of the blaze, but it has not yet been identified." Gregson paused again, not actually knowing how he felt, apart from empty. "So what happened?" he asked.

"It says in the article that they don't know," was the policeman's reply.

"But?" Gregson could sense the other man was holding something back.

"They found massive traces of accelerant," Townshend said.

"And that means?"

"It means someone deliberately set fire to your house, Mr. Gregson. Now why would someone want to do that?"

"I have no idea." And truly he didn't.

"No enemies? No one you've upset recently?"

"No. I don't tend to have arguments with people," Gregson replied. "You didn't come all the way to Canterbury to ask me about my house, did you?" he asked after another pause in the conversation. "Come to that, how did you know I was here? And how did you know where I was just at this moment?" His voice was rising, his indignation all too apparent. Several passers by looked around at the two men.

"For someone who doesn't like arguments, you seem to be getting quite angry, Mr. Gregson. Are you still taking your medication?" Gregson had been taking tablets for longer than he could remember, mainly to keep him calm and stop bad dreams.

"What do you know about that?" he asked. Townshend smiled.

"I know about your whereabouts and your medication because I'm a good policeman, Mr. Gregson. If you care to remember, you have been questioned about a murder case and a related apparent missing person. I asked Canterbury police to keep an eye on you."

"It seems that everyone is keeping an eye on me," Gregson muttered angrily to himself.

"Sorry? I didn't quite catch that," said the detective.

"Nothing, just thinking aloud. Do you know someone called Blakeley?"

"No. Should I?"

"It seemed possible." Gregson paused thoughtfully. He still felt uncomfortable around policemen and there was something about all this that didn't add up properly. Holding the newspaper, he repeated his question. "You didn't come here just to show me this, did you?" The detective smiled, but in a way Gregson wasn't too sure he liked.

"Have you seen the castle ruins, Mr. Gregson? It was the first castle William the Conqueror had built in England after the battle of Hastings. It's quite interesting. Shall we take a short walk?" Both men rose from their seats and strolled down the path past the mound Gregson had climbed earlier. He looked up, half expecting to see Blakeley watching him, but there was no one there.

"A new piece of information, call it evidence if you prefer, has come to light concerning the murder of the young woman who was for some reason carrying Sonia Fox's handbag," the DI said as they walked.

"Why would that concern me?" Gregson asked.

"Because it's actually the reason I'm here to see you, Mr. Gregson. Another bag, a shoulder bag, nowhere near the same quality as Mrs. Fox's, was found in the reeds near the scene. We believe it was the bag that really belonged to the victim." Another pause, a habit of the detective's that was starting to annoy Gregson.

"And?"

"Among the contents of this second bag was a piece of paper with your name and address on it." Gregson stopped in mid stride and turned to look at him.

"What?" they'd just reached the gates to the park, and Townshend directed him to a footpath on the other side of the road alongside a car park.

"The castle is this way," he said, apparently ignoring Gregson's exclamation, but then returning to it once they were safely across the road. "Now, it does seem rather strange that a young woman is seemingly attacked and murdered carrying the handbag of another woman who looks as if she has disappeared, doesn't it? And then of course, you were supposed to be meeting the missing woman for dinner and your name and address were in a bag found with the murder victim. There does seem to be a connection there, don't you think?" Gregson didn't know what to think.

"Has the victim been identified?" he asked, hoping that might give him some sort of clue. The detective nodded. They crossed another road to the entrance to the castle, of which only the central keep remained standing.

"Let's go inside," Townshend suggested. "There are seats inside, and castles really are an interest of mine." As they seated themselves in what was effectively a huge stone box open to the sky, Townshend continued. "The second bag allowed us to make a positive identification. Her name was Tara Colman. Mean anything?" He watched Gregson closely for any sign of recognition. There was none. Gregson couldn't place the name, desperate though he was to try to make some sense out of this, some connection. "There was a photograph which further confirmed that identification." He pulled a picture from his jacket, a copy of the original. "Does she look familiar?" Again the detective was watching him closely, and Gregson's heart sank as he looked at the smiling face. Only she hadn't been smiling quite so much when he'd met her for the first and only time. "I take it you do recognise her. You wouldn't make a very good poker player you know, Mr Gregson."

"No, probably not," Gregson agreed, still looking at the picture and finding it hard to believe that the girl was dead. "Yes, I have met this young woman, only once and that was briefly and in a slightly embarrassing situation. But I had no idea of her name."

He passed the photograph back, aware of his hands feeling rather clammy, a sensation which had nothing to do with the weather.

"So what's the link?"

"There is no link," replied Gregson.

"But you did say that you have met her?" The question was quite insistent.

"Yes." Gregson went on to explain the embarrassing circumstances in The Bomb on the evening of his wife's funeral.

"That would explain another of the items found in Tara Colman's handbag," said the policeman. "There was a dry cleaning slip for an uncollected garment." Gregson felt a pang of sadness for the young woman, for a short life unfulfilled. There was a very long pause, during which he had the feeling that the detective was searching for his next question. "Mr. Gregson, I have the feeling that something rather strange is going on and at the moment it all seems to revolve around you. The only other option is a bizarre set of coincidences and I won't accept that. Why are you in Canterbury, Mr. Gregson, and not at home?" The question was unexpected. Gregson sighed.

"I came to meet someone."

"Please don't make this difficult, Mr. Gregson. Just who was it you were meeting?"

"Sonia Fox." There was no reaction form Townshend, almost as if it was what he had been expecting.

"Did she turn up?"

"No."

"A rather elusive lady, Mrs. Fox, isn't she?" The DI leaned forward a little, smiling, his chin in his hands and his elbows resting on his knees. Gregson noticed it was beginning to turn a bit chilly in the shade of the keep. Then Townshend spoke again, without looking up. "For someone whom you've not seen for twenty years, Mrs. Fox suddenly seems to be playing a very important part in your life, doesn't she?" Gregson had to agree.

"She told me she needed help and that she would explain when I met her here in Canterbury," he said.

"So someone in need of help stood up her gallant knight in shining armour – twice," said the DI. Gregson made no reply, a little put out by the policeman's sarcastic tone. "And you say you've no idea of what help she needs?" the detective persisted.

"No. She said she'd explain when we met," Gregson repeated. Townshend was silent for a few moments.

"Mr. Gregson, I have to be frank here. Given your unfortunately deep involvement in this case, I've had to do extensive background checking on you, and you just don't strike me as the type of person these things happen to. I don't understand at all, and I don't like not understanding." Gregson didn't think it would help matters to say he didn't understand either. "You mentioned a name earlier," the detective suddenly asked.

"Yes. Keith Blakeley."

"What's he got to do with all this? You didn't explain."

"He says he needs to find Sonia, that she turned to him for help."

"It certainly sounds like our Mrs. Fox needs a lot of help," Townshend said drily. "What did this Blakeley tell you about himself?"

"He gave me the impression he works for the government."

"For the government? Is there anything more?"

"More?"

"Yes. Any other names or people I should be interested in."

"No names, but someone else is involved. There was a woman who followed me from home to Canterbury Cathedral. I got away from her when she told me Sonia wasn't coming."

"She knew that?"

"Apparently, yes. And she told me I had to go with her for a 'quiet chat'," he added as an afterthought. There was another long pause and he noticed a very concerned look cross the detective's face.

"This all sounds like something you became involved in by accident, Mr. Gregson. My advice to you is to forget your noble motives about helping Mrs Fox and simply go home."

"What home?" Gregson asked, the question reminding the suddenly apologetic looking detective that it had been burned down. "I think it's gone beyond walking away." Gregson's words and resolve surprised him almost as much as they did the DI.

"People who burn down houses don't tend to be very friendly, Mr. Gregson. Staying involved may not be the brightest thing to do. Find somewhere quiet to go for a while."

"Detective Inspector, I can't see anyway of not staying involved. I'm not happy about it, but I think that's the reality of the situation." The DI nodded and reached into his pocket, pulling out a Cambridgeshire Constabulary business card. He scribbled a number on the back.

"That's my personal mobile number. If anything strange happens, get in touch."

"There's a lot going on here that I don't understand," Gregson said. "How do I know I can trust you anymore than I can anyone else?"

"That, unfortunately, is a decision you have to make for yourself, Mr. Gregson."

CHAPTER NINE

Gregson played the detective's words over and over in his mind after the two men had parted. He was walking back to his hotel to collect his belongings and check out, conscious that there were three groups of people anxious to find Sonia Fox, and that two of them were relying on him to lead them to her. Despite what he'd said about not seeing how he could avoid being involved, it wasn't that hard for him to decide to follow the detective's advice and find somewhere quiet for a short break, and he knew just the place. The hotel he was staying at, more of a guest house really, was only a short walk from Canterbury West railway station and he intended to be on the first London-bound train available. As far as trusting the detective went, that was another matter. As he'd he told him, he wasn't sure who, if anyone, he could trust.

Just about to walk across the gravelled parking spaces outside his hotel, he heard a squeal of brakes behind him and the screech of tyres on the road. Human nature being what it is he turned to see what was going on, expecting to hear the metallic thump of two cars hitting each other. Instead, he saw only one car, a large one with blacked out windows. Without even a chance to think about what was happening, he was bundled into the back of the car, with something being pulled over his head, plunging him into darkness. His arms were pulled together and he heard and felt handcuffs being fastened tightly on his wrists. The car then pulled away quickly with another screech of tyres. He couldn't breathe properly, but he did catch the scent of a flowery perfume he recognised with a sinking heart. Not being able to see or hear anything clearly quickly brought on a feeling of nausea when combined with the motion of the car.

The rapid motion of the car lasted only a few minutes before it stopped suddenly and he was thrown from the back seat to the floor. Then it moved forward more slowly, with a different sensation as if driving over gravel. Then it stopped again and this time the engine was turned off. He was dragged unceremoniously out of the vehicle, and then hauled away, feeling gravel scrunch under his shoes, and then a harder, more solid surface, before being forced roughly down some steps. He lost his footing, almost going to his knees, being prevented from doing so by the firm grip of his captors. Colliding with what he took to be a door frame, he was guided to a seat, to which he was then tied, painfully and securely. As far as he could tell, he was then left alone, with a growing headache and arms that were becoming increasingly numb from being fastened so uncomfortably behind him. There was only one thing he was sure of – he was scared, very scared. It seemed an age that he was on his own, if indeed he was. He became more tense, the headache growing, and the fear of what might be happening was overwhelming. That this had something to do with Sonia he had no doubt. Claustrophobia inside the hood began to add to his problems and he tried to control his rising panic by slow, deep breathing, but it didn't seem to work. Whatever material had been used for the hood began to cling to his face alarmingly. Shallow breaths seemed better, but still time dragged on.

Somehow, he must have slept or lapsed into unconsciousness, being jerked awake by rough hands on his shoulders. He was untied, made to stand on suddenly weak legs and the handcuffs were removed from his wrists. Despite the pain in his arms and the discomfort of the blood flowing back into his hands, he instinctively tried to reach up to rid himself of the cloying hood. A sharp command stopped him.

"No, leave it, Mr. Gregson." He knew that voice and something in its tone made him obey immediately. He lowered his arms back down to his sides. In addition to the muffling caused by the hood, her voice, that of the woman in the cathedral, sounded amplified or distorted in some way. But it was definitely her and something in her tone left little room for argument. He stood and waited. And waited. Then the voice, filled with authority and the confidence of being in control, barked again. "Take off your clothes." Through the hood, Gregson wasn't sure if he'd heard properly.

"What?" he said through the fabric, his mouth parched and dry. Just how long had he been there, he asked himself. A swift painful punch to his left kidney forced him to his knees. He was pulled immediately back to his feet.

"Take off your clothes," the voice repeated. Reluctantly, and taking as long as he possibly could, Gregson did so, until finally he was standing naked and vulnerable, the hood over his head his only covering. He sensed movement around him, but no one spoke for a long time. That faint flowery perfume hung in the air again. She was close and then she spoke, undistorted, clear as a bell.

"Mr. Gregson, I was very disappointed by your behaviour in the cathedral. And very surprised by your audacity." She sounded like a schoolteacher reprimanding a naughty pupil. "Now, to explain, we are looking for something, and we have not found it in your clothes." There was a long pause which gave him the chance to consider what she'd just said. They were looking for an object, not Sonia Fox herself. But before he had a chance to think about it further, she continued. "I'm going to have you searched. Do you understand? Just nod your head." Gregson nodded. He'd heard about full body searches and didn't relish the idea, not that he had much choice. Two pairs of hands grabbed his arms and forced him to the floor, spread eagled. The next few minutes were a period of his life he was sure he'd never be able to make himself forget. The concrete floor was cold, hard and unforgiving, particularly with a boot on the back of his neck forcing his cheek into it. His hands and legs were also pinned to the floor. But it was the indignity and intrusiveness of the search and the probing fingers which appalled him. Shaking, he was dragged to his feet once more. The woman spoke again, but Gregson was only half listening to what she was saying.

"Mrs. Fox has something I want, something I am being paid handsomely to retrieve. I was given the impression that it had possibly been passed on to you, but it wasn't in your house, nor in your luggage or your hotel room. And as we've now discovered, it isn't in your clothes or anywhere about your person. That disappoints me and I don't like being disappointed. I'm going to ask you a question, which I sincerely hope you have the good sense to answer truthfully. Has Mrs. Fox given you anything to keep for her? Something she's told you not to tell anyone about? Think carefully before you answer. I have a knack for rooting out lies." Gregson slowly and deliberately shook his head. There was no response other than a long pause. Then she said, speaking to someone else, "Deal with him." He felt a sharp stab of pain in his thigh and collapsed to the floor.

CHAPTER TEN

Something must have woken him, some noise or movement that only dimly registered in his mind, but on opening his eyes, he immediately wished he was still asleep. Groggy though he was, the light was almost blinding, white, bright and clinical. He closed his eyes to get away from it, fighting extreme nausea and a hangover like headache. He was in a bed, he realised, head raised on a pile of pillows with a soft humming noise in the background. He cautiously opened his eyes again and saw he was lying in a hospital bed and across the room, dozing on what looked like a very uncomfortable chair, was Detective Inspector Townshend. Gregson coughed gently to wake him and a sharp pain around his kidneys made him regret it. The policeman woke instantly.

"What's going on and what am I doing here?" Gregson asked groggily.

"Well, you're in hospital, Mr Gregson," the DI began, stating what Gregson had already worked out.

"How did I get here?" He remembered all too well the events that had led up to his unconsciousness, but nothing more. He felt rather uneasy as a broad grin spread across the detectives face.

"Two WPCs found you," he said, "in the early hours of this morning."

"Found me? Where?"

"On the ring road, lying on the grass verge. Strangely, you were wearing a hood and you were handcuffed. You were also stark naked, which led them to believe…"

"I can guess what it led them to believe," Gregson interrupted.

"Well, anyway," Townshend continued, the grin staying broad at Gregson's discomfort, "your clothes and belongings were in a pile next to you. One of the WPCs found the business card I gave you yesterday. The smile disappeared and Townshend leaned forward in his chair. "Are you going to tell me what happened?" Gregson slumped back on his pillows and tried not to think about being found by the two WPCs. He groaned slightly, and then told the DI everything, staring upwards at the ceiling and not looking at him.

"You say they searched your hotel room?" Townshend asked.

"So she said."

"Well, it's a long shot because they sound like professionals, but it might be worth checking for prints and having a chat with the owners." Gregson gave him details of the hotel and asked for his bags to be brought to the hospital. When the detective left the room, he sank gratefully back into sleep. By the time Townshend returned much later in the day, Gregson felt much better.

"Have they said when you can leave?" the DI asked him.

"Apparently the doctor wants to keep me in for another night for further observation. They're not sure what was used to knock me out, or how much of it was pumped into me."

"Good. You'll be safe here, and I'll leave a man on the door, but I don't think you're in any danger."

"No?" said Gregson, in the most sarcastic tone he could manage. "And just what makes you think that?"

"Because I think who ever abducted you wants you to lead them to Sonia Fox, Mr. Gregson. It's when you actually find her that you'll be in danger." Townshend paused, as if waiting for a reaction from Gregson, but none came. "As far as this thing they want, have you any idea what it is, or how big it might be?" Gregson looked at him and laughed.

"Well, Detective Inspector, I'm pretty sure it's not very big," he said sourly. Townshend appeared disconcerted.

"Why?" he asked.

"Because they think it's small enough to fit up my backside."

"Ah. Good point."

"And no, I don't know what it is or what it might be. All I know, like I've told you, is that Sonia asked for my help."

"Mm." The detective didn't sound convinced. "I'll leave you to rest. Your things are all in the bag," he added, gesturing towards the bag on the chair.

"What about my hotel room?" Gregson asked.

"Clean as a whistle. The chamber maid had beaten us to it. Your bag had been packed and left at reception to be collected, and, you'll be pleased to hear you bill had been paid." And, thought the DI sourly, the CCTV in reception hadn't been working, and no one could give a description of who'd done it. But he didn't mention it.

"Paid?"

"Yes, in full. Strange, isn't it?" he paused, gauging Gregson's reaction. "I'll be in to see you in the morning for another chat before you're discharged." He crossed the room to the door. "The other thing that's strange of course is that a woman who so many people seem anxious to find has not been registered as a missing person with the police, even though she's apparently disappeared." He left before Gregson had a chance to say anything, not that he had anything he could say.

When the morning came, after a fitful nights sleep, Gregson had decided not to wait for either the doctor or the detective to come back. After eating his breakfast, he dressed and discharged himself, ignoring the protests of the nurses and the policeman on duty. Taking a bus from the hospital to the railway station, he was already on a high speed train back to St. Pancras by the time DI Townshend arrived at the hospital.

CHAPTER ELEVEN

DI Townshend wasn't at all amused that Malcolm Gregson had discharged himself from the hospital, impressed as he was that he'd done it. He didn't honestly think that the man had the balls for such an act. Gregson did however strike him as an ordinary man who didn't know who he could trust and who'd found himself in a far from ordinary situation. Townshend was having problems with this case himself. What had started as a simple murder case, if a murder could ever be described as simple, was becoming increasingly complicated and confusing.

A career policeman, Townshend lived for his job. He had what he considered a highly developed sense of right and wrong despite being all too aware of the many shades of grey that life was more than happy to throw up. His passion for his job had cost him too many relationships, including two failed marriages, for which he felt no bitterness towards his ex–wives. Thankfully, in both cases, there had been no children involved.

He ran one hand through a tousled mass of ginger hair. This case was perplexing. Was Tara Colman a victim of a bungled mugging? The area her body was found in was notorious for theft and assault. Had something gone wrong when somebody tried to steal a handbag? No. The problem was two handbags, one belonging to the victim and thrown into the reeds, and one belonging to the mysterious Sonia Fox. A coincidence? Again, no. As he'd explained to Malcolm Gregson, the DI didn't believe in coincidences. They were too easy, too convenient. There was a reason. There had to be a reason. How had Tara Colman actually been in possession of two handbags? Had she stolen it? Perhaps she'd found it. A thought occurred to him, and he picked up his phone. It rang only twice at the other end before being answered.

"DC Miller. Can I help?"

"Rob, it's Townshend. A question for you."

"Yes sir? Rob Miller had worked with DI Townshend for some years and always enjoyed his superior's absences from the office.

"The handbag that was found with Tara Colman."

"The one belonging to Mrs. Fox?"

"Yes. Was it checked for prints? I don't recall seeing the report."

"I'll check, sir. Can I ring you back?"

"Yes, Rob. On my mobile, if you would." Townshend knew Miller wouldn't be long in returning his call, and continued to think while he was waiting. When he found himself drumming his fingers on the table, he leaned back in his chair, clasped his hands behind his head and forced himself to relax. He was still in the same position ten minutes later when his mobile rang.

"Yes, Rob?"

"Sorry about the delay. For some reason the report had already been filed. The bag was clean, sir. No prints on it at all."

"None?"

"No, sir. None at all."

"Doesn't that strike you as strange, Rob?"

"Strange? Why, sir?"

"No prints at all, not even Sonia Fox's?" The DI asked. There was a slight pause.

"It's been wiped?"

"It certainly looks that way. What about the other bag, the one belonging to the girl?" There was a rustle of papers.

"Same thing, sir. Completely clean. Oh, sir, there is one other thing," said Miller.

"Yes?"

"The autopsy report is back on the Colman girl."

"About bloody time. Anything interesting?"

"A lot of bruising indicates quite a hectic struggle, so I think she might have put up a bit of a fight, and there's a single needle-mark in her thigh but no other indications that she might have been a drug user. It's a bit suspicious and toxicology are still working on their report."

"A needle-mark? See if you can hurry them along a bit, would you?"

"Yes, sir," the needle mark gave Townshend pause for thought. Malcolm Gregson had been injected with something in the thigh. Another coincidence?

"Cause of death?"

"They're still working on that, but the thinking is that it has something to do with that needle-mark, sir." The DI sighed quietly. "Doesn't smack of the average mugger does it, sir?"

"No, Rob, it looks a lot more professional. But why?"

"My first thought would be rape, sir, but there's no evidence of sexual assault."

"I agree, but that still leaves us with why. Why was a young woman drugged, presumably to sedate her, and then neither robbed or raped?"

"Maybe the attacker got scared when she died?" Rob said.

"But would she have died immediately, or just not come round from the effects of the drug?" mused the DI. There was a long pause at the other end of the phone.

"I don't know, sir," said Rob.

"Nor do I, Rob, but hopefully we'll have more of an idea when toxicology get back to us. Thanks for the good work." He ended the call with a request that his subordinate ring him as soon as he

74

had any more information. Then he sat back to think again. Both Tara Colman and Malcolm Gregson had been injected with some sort of sedative and both in the thigh. Coincidence? He thought not. And there was a tenuous link between the two of them over the spilled drink. Not much to go on there. He carried on thinking. What was it Gregson had said to him in the hospital? Oh yes, that the doctors weren't sure what he'd been injected with. He picked up his phone, rang the hospital and was put through to the duty doctor, who unfortunately wasn't the same doctor who'd originally treated Malcolm Gregson.

"It's not a problem, Detective Inspector," the doctor said. "I can easily call up Mr Gregson's record for you if you give me a few moments." Townshend could hear the taping of a computer keyboard. "Mr. Gregson discharged himself this morning, Detective Inspector. Is that right?" Townshend confirmed that it was. "Right, here we are. Blood tests showed abnormal levels of sedative when he was admitted."

"What was it?" the DI asked.

"What was what? The doctor asked.

"The actual sedative. What was it?" Townshend tried not to sound as irritated as he felt.

"Oh, right. It was Propofol."

"Is that easily available?"

"Oh God, no. It's only used in surgery." There was a pause while Townshend digested that piece of information.

"Just one more question, doctor. What happens if it mixes with alcohol?"

"You mean if it's accidentally given to someone who's been drinking?"

"Yes. What's likely to be the outcome?"

"It would be really bad news. There's only one outcome, you see. It would almost certainly be fatal." After ending the phone call, Townshend sat and pondered a long time.

He was becoming both angry and disappointed. Angry with himself, and disappointed in Malcolm Gregson. He should have expected Gregson to run: in his position he would probably have done the same thing. But now he had no idea where the man was.

Gregson was the key to all this, a central character, if only because he was the only person with whom Sonia Fox was in contact. The abduction in Canterbury had been a shock for Gregson, a glimpse into a world he was unfamiliar with, and despite his detached attitude, the detective felt sorry for him. But it was evidence that there was something very serious connected with the disappearance of Sonia Fox.

His investigations were proceeding slowly, but after his last two phone calls he was now convinced that Tara Colman's death wasn't a premeditated act or a failed mugging but was basically fall out from a larger situation. The poor girl had been in the wrong place at the wrong time. It was simply that Propofol and alcohol were a lethal combination and the best he would be able to hope for, should he ever find the perpetrator, was a manslaughter charge. It was the Propofol that worried him. A powerful general anaesthetic, it was used to put patients under for operations and should only be administered by qualified health professionals who knew what they were doing. Not only should it only be administered by them, it should also only be available to them. It seemed unlikely that such a professional would be involved with doping and abductions, but not beyond the realms of possibility. The question was where was it coming from and who was using it? The answers to those questions might be a long time coming, if they came at all. It was an easy decision to make to put them out of his mind for the time being, but not such an easy thing to do. The matter disturbed him.

CHAPTER TWELVE

Gregson was on a bus again, this time travelling down the Golden Valley in Herefordshire, far away from Canterbury. He felt like he was playing games, but sensed that the detective's advice, to find somewhere to hide, was right. He felt vaguely guilty about slipping away from the hospital when he knew that the DI was coming to see him, but he was in no mood to face any more questions for which he had no answers.

The bus journey was just another part of the game, but one that seemed interminable, despite the attraction of the scenery. He was worried to the point of paranoia about being followed, so he'd chosen the bus rather than use his credit card to hire a car. He'd seen enough films to know that credit card transactions could be traced easily by someone with the wherewithal and the correct equipment. However, he hadn't considered that the same could be said for cash machine withdrawals, and that now worried him.

The bus was noisy and full, and the voices of two girls in the seat immediately behind him began to intrude on his thoughts. A chit chat conversation of no depth, carried on in high pitched voices, it seemed to carry right through the bus and irritated him immediately. He wanted to think and a crowded bus wasn't the best place. It didn't help that the rest of the passengers on the bus were probably feeling the same way because of the volume of the one everyone was being forced to listen to.

"Did you go out on Saturday?"

"Yes, with Sean and Jonathan. I was only going to have the one drink, but I ended up doing a pub crawl with them. Literally, I mean. I could hardly walk."

"Yeah, I got hammered as well." Gregson sighed to himself and suddenly felt very, very sad. These two girls, both in their early twenties, were around the same age as the murdered girl, Tara Colman. For some reason, he felt responsible, a feeling of unexplained guilt he couldn't shake off. But, he told himself, it was more to do with Sonia Fox than him, wasn't it? The conversation continued.

"Where'd you go?"

"In the Blue Boar in Hay. You been in there?"

"Used to go in there, but not now." And so on and so on and so on. The whole bus seemed to go quiet while this conversation was going on, until Gregson's mobile phone rang, breaking the spell of interest and normal conversations resumed around him. Another unknown number, something he was growing increasingly used to. He pressed 'busy'. It rang again, and he did the same thing and considered turning it off. Then a text message arrived and with a sigh he opened it. 'Malcolm. Pls ans phone. Sonia. xx' He turned the phone off, putting it in his jacket pocket.

When the bus stopped in Hay-on-Wye the two girls, still talking far too loudly, disembarked much to the relief of the remaining passengers. He fingered his phone, now feeling doubly guilty. But he'd decided, while lying in his hospital bed, with nothing else to do but think, that if he could somehow manage it, he wanted nothing more to do with whatever was going on. He was quite simply at a loss to understand everything that had happened so quickly to his well-ordered, routine and frankly boring life since his wife had died.

He was on his way to a bed and breakfast in the small town of Talgarth in the Black Mountains just over the border between England and Wales, a lovely place he'd stayed at before in past years, escaping from his wife, and no one knew where he was going. As far as he knew, no one had followed him from Canterbury and the only headache he had was his mobile phone, because it seemed that everyone who was looking for Sonia knew the number. He could ditch it, but couldn't bring himself to. Annoyingly, his fingers kept finding their way to the 'on/off' button, but he resisted the temptation to turn it on.

When the bus stopped in the small market place of Talgarth, opposite the old tower which now housed the town's Tourist Information Office, Gregson grabbed his small suitcase and climbed down, gratefully stretching his legs. The bed and breakfast was up a steep hill, beyond the church and the brief but strenuous walk left him out of breath. He rang the door bell and surprised though they were to see him, he had a lovely warm welcome from Gwen and Phil McNally, the couple who ran the business. Luckily they had a room, and after a short chat where they sympathised about the loss of his wife, they left him to it, and he relaxed on the bed. Unpacking his few belongings could come a little later.

The more he lay gazing at the ceiling, the more his curiosity grew about the text he'd received on the bus. From Sonia, on an unknown number. Rising from the bed, he retrieved the phone from his jacket, and turned it on, safe in the knowledge that he would get no phone signal here, because he never had, and it was one of the reasons he liked coming back. He opened the message again. It seemed harmless enough, but was it Sonia, or was it one of Keith Blakeley's tricks to try to try to find him? One thing was for sure, he wasn't going to ring the number back, nor was he going to answer if it rang again when he had a signal. But it might be safe to reply by text just to see if he could work out who it was. Tomorrow, he decided, he'd take a walk and do just that.

The morning light, when it finally came, didn't help with his decision and the old saying of 'everything always looks better in the morning' wasn't working for him. It had been a restless night's sleep but now, outside, it was a gorgeous morning, worthy of a summer's day, and the sunshine slowly brought him fully awake. He stretched lazily and managed to rouse himself sufficiently to make it to the en-suite shower room. The shower refreshed him and gave him an appetite for breakfast, and, having sampled Gwen McNally's breakfasts before, he knew he was going to enjoy it.

Gwen, having heard him moving about, already had coffee waiting for him on the table.

"Is it a full breakfast for you this morning, Malcolm?" she asked.

"Yes, please," he said, already helping himself to cereal. He'd just sat down when his mobile phone beeped in his pocket. He took it out and looked at it. A text message. He looked at Gwen, puzzled. "I've never been able to get a signal here before. Has something changed?"

"Oh, yes. People raised such a fuss about not being able to use their phones that something was done to improve it. Don't ask me what, though. I don't understand these things and neither Phil nor me will have anything to do with mobile telephones. I have enough trouble with   e-mails," she laughed. Gregson felt both disappointed and irritated but opened the text anyway and then swore under his breath. 'Mr. Gregson. Have you heard from our mutual friend Sonia? How's the weather in Wales? Blakeley.' How the hell did he know?

He typed in 'No' and went back to his breakfast, unsettled and nervous.

CHAPTER THIRTEEN

Joseph Fox found dead. That wasn't very good news, Townshend thought sourly to himself. The phone call from Miller had upset his breakfast, and had without a doubt further complicated things. His colleagues at Scotland Yard were treating it as a suspicious death, Miller had said, but no details had been released yet. Townshend's department had only been informed because of the dead man's sister being involved in a current murder investigation they were carrying out. Townshend swore. For God's sake, he was only on his second cup of coffee this morning.

The question that now bothered him was quite simple. Was Joseph Fox killed because someone wanted to find his sister Sonia? Had she disappeared because of some danger to the pair of them? And of course the question that kept coming back like the proverbial bad penny: Was Malcolm Gregson involved somehow? He absently poured himself another coffee, adding far too much cream with only a slight pang of guilt. Taking a sip, he mentally reviewed what he knew about Fox, the background information his team had uncovered in the course of their investigation. The man was an investment broker, a glorified name for a wheeler dealer. He'd been involved in dodgy deals, but nothing that could even loosely be described as illegal, but playing with large amounts of other people's money at the murky end of the business world could be dangerous, particularly if you made mistakes or became a little greedy. There were a lot of people who could be very unforgiving of mistakes involving their money. He took another sip of coffee.

The Detective Inspector wasn't the only person who had been unsettled by the death of Joseph Fox. Keith Blakeley was alternating between an explosive fury and raging frustration, with his office staff trying their hardest to keep out of his way. His secretary in particular was on edge, having been in and out of his office with various files. Relieved that he seemed to be quiet at the moment, she was taking advantage of the opportunity of having a much needed cup of tea. Blakeley was actually gazing out of his office window watching pigeons crowding each other off the window ledges on the building opposite, his mind busy.

For Blakeley, Joseph Fox being murdered, and Blakeley had no doubt that it was murder, was a real problem. He'd wanted the man alive, because at least that way he might have been able to get some information out of him. Ironically, it had been Fox's sister Sonia who'd contacted Blakeley's department about her brother's activities, saying she had proof he was having shady dealings with Chinese investors and she was concerned the Chinese government were behind it. Her status as a high-ranking government officer gave credence to her worries as far as Blakeley was concerned and had grabbed his attention. It fitted within his department, his area of responsibility and his personal passion for geopolitics.

As he was fond of explaining to anyone unfortunate enough to be within earshot, geopolitics, is the study of recent historical events and forecasting future events based on the conflicts between rival cultures and Blakeley was considered to be a leading government expert in the field. China with its ever-increasing population already exceeding a quarter of humanity and with its economy growing almost as fast, is a major player and consequently of interest to Blakeley. The theory behind it all is that civilisations and cultures are always seeking to expand and develop and while in the past this was always through war and conquest, it is now through economic superiority. Blakeley always liked to quote a speech from a Russian Defence Minister, one Pavel Grachev, where the man had said "The Chinese are in the process of making a peaceful conquest of the Russian Far East."

Blakeley knew that certain members of his department regarded his worries about China as verging on paranoia and there was an element of hope that his theories might be vindicated by whatever evidence Sonia Fox had discovered. He was certain that the already high level of Chinese investment in the United Kingdom was more than matched by covert investment, leading to a situation whereby the Chinese might be pursuing a 'peaceful conquest' of British industry. Now he had a problem in that Sonia Fox had gone missing in possession of the evidence he so badly wanted and the man he was desperate to question was dead. Joseph Fox might well have been able to give the answers to some interesting questions.

Still, what was done was done, and he wasn't the sort of person to dwell too long on mistakes or 'might have beens.' It was now imperative for him to find Sonia Fox and with her the proof he so badly needed; it looked like the only way to do that seemed to be through Malcolm Gregson. But he was bothered as to why Sonia Fox had turned to Gregson for help. It didn't make sense.

There was one other person who was well aware of Joseph Fox's death, the person who'd actually killed him. Cara Bingham had followed Gregson to Canterbury and had abducted and subsequently released him, hoping to use him to trace Sonia Fox. She regarded herself as a freelance and this current contract was lucrative, very lucrative, as well as being, on the surface, relatively straightforward. Find and eliminate Joseph Fox and find his sister and the evidence she had; once the evidence of Joseph Fox's misdeeds was secure in Cara's possession, Sonia Fox was also to be eliminated. The greedy investment broker had been dealt with satisfactorily and much to her disappointment, far too easily, but Cara was hopeful that dealing with Sonia Fox would be much more enjoyable.

While Townshend was thoughtfully drinking his coffee and Blakeley abstractedly gazing at pigeons, Cara Bingham was in a branch of WH Smith looking at books and waiting for a contact.

Too much has been written about the deadly and beautiful female assassin, Cara thought sourly, browsing through the novels in the shop display. Beauty and elegance always attract attention, particularly in a woman. Attention was the last thing an assassin needed. Then she laughed to herself. Well, she was in a position to know, wasn't she? Cara was well aware that she was a plain ordinary looking woman and had been that way since she was a little girl. And she was an assassin, a very good one, according to her various employers. She was also still very much alive, which was of course, in her profession, a real sign of success.

And that was why she was looking forward to finding and dealing with Sonia Fox, the epitome of the beautiful assassin. However the woman might be described in her role for the British Government and it certainly wouldn't be that, it was what Cara knew her to be. The two women had only crossed paths once, but that had given them a history which gave a personal edge to Cara's search. She smiled again. Sonia Fox was an added bonus to an already generous fee from her current employers.

CHAPTER FOURTEEN

Walking gives time for thinking, and time to get his thoughts in order was what Gregson needed. A display of tourist leaflets in the McNally's hallway gave him a purpose to his walk, with a short history of four towers in the immediate area of Talgarth. Before stepping out, he took a few minutes to look at the details of the walk. The first tower was down in the town centre and now housed the tourist information office and Gregson was damned if he was going to walk all the way down that steep hill from where he was just to walk back up to the nearby church which was the second tower. Pulling on his coat and making sure his mobile was charged, he decided to start at the church.

It was by now mid-morning and there were few people about at this upper end of the town, apart from an elderly man tidying a grave by the churchyard wall, who looked up and gave Gregson a cheery wave as he walked past. Along the lane towards some houses, the directions took Gregson away from the town and out into a grassy track which finally led out into a field. He finally felt alone and began to attempt to make some sense of the confusion in his mind.

There was a reason Sonia Fox had involved him in whatever was going on; there had to be or nothing would make any sense. His actions in the hotel had been totally out of character and there had been something nagging at him about the chambermaid who'd passed him the note. She'd called him Mr. Greenhill. He'd thought nothing of it at the time, but ever since there had been something tugging at his mind, a thought or a memory just far enough out of reach that he couldn't quite grasp it. It was something elusive that he felt should be so familiar.

Reaching a stile, he climbed over quickly, checking carefully that there was nobody following and ensuring there was no one ahead. An image of being chased flashed into his mind combined with the fear of being caught and he felt suddenly dizzy and grabbed hold of the stile for support. There was the sound of shouting and dogs, angry, snarling creatures, in his ears, but when he looked around, he was on his own in the corner of a field by a stile.

He sat down on the grass. What had that been all about? It seemed so real, so vivid, almost as if it had actually happened to him. He almost laughed out loud. How could something like that happen to a simple man like him? After a few minutes, but still feeling a little shaken, he got back to his feet and continued along the footpath. He was heading for the third tower on the walk, a gateway to an old farmhouse and trying to focus his thoughts on Sonia.

Gregson was worried that Keith Blakeley knew where he was, and equally worried about Blakeley's involvement in the whole affair. He was sure the man was holding something back from him. The footpath took him out of the fields and along the main road towards Hay-on-Wye, then down through a farmyard without him even noticing the gate tower indicated on the walk while his mind struggled with the problem of Sonia Fox.

She was the only person who could explain to him what was going on and why he'd been involved, and he was avoiding her. By the time he emerged on the Talgarth to Bronllys road, he'd decided to reply to her message. He needed answers and she was obviously the key. A text or should he phone her? Could Blakeley intercept texts or could he just trace mobile phones? It didn't matter really. The man seemed to have the technology to do what he wanted, so let him. I'll deal with that problem when it comes up, Gregson thought, if I can.

Seeing a footpath leading towards Bronllys Castle, he turned in and in a few seconds found himself looking up at all that remained, a round tower on the hillside with what seemed like an inordinate number of steps leading up to it. The ruins didn't seem to be very well visited, so he decided to remain at the base of the mound, where it was nice and secluded, and took his mobile from his coat. He looked at it for some time before selecting Sonia's number from his contact list. He felt apprehensive about this, as if he was taking a major step towards something without quite knowing what it was.

He pushed the number.

"Malcolm? Is that you?" It was definitely Sonia's voice.

"Hello, Sonia." He paused.

"Where are you, Malcolm? I was starting to think you're avoiding me," she said. He suddenly felt very defensive.

"Do you really need to know, Sonia? It seems to be you who's avoiding me." This time the pause was at Sonia's end.

"We need to meet," she said eventually.

"You've said that before, but you've not told me why." Another pause. He wished he knew what she was thinking. Since the hotel incident and the events in Canterbury he'd become convinced she was holding something back, but couldn't quite work out where that suspicious side to his nature had come from. It wasn't part of the Malcolm Gregson he thought he was.

"I certainly owe you an explanation, Malcolm, but not on the phone." Sonia sounded conciliatory. "When we meet I'll tell you what's going on, but you might not necessarily like it." Gregson felt he had no choice.

"All right Sonia, but this is the last time. Where do you want to meet?"

"That depends on where you are."

"Near Brecon in Wales," he replied. There was another pause and he assumed she was working something out at her end.

"Do you know the Elan Valley Reservoirs? They're near Rhayader on the edge of the Cambrian mountains."

"No," replied Gregson, "but I can find out."

"There's a disused church at the top end of the lowest reservoir by the aqueduct. It's called Nantygwltt. Meet me on the green hill. Three o'clock tomorrow afternoon." She disconnected the call without a goodbye.

A church on a green hill, he thought to himself. That shouldn't be too hard to find. A sudden thought occurred to him: why stress a green hill? There would be a lot of those in Wales. Why did he keep thinking there was something familiar about those words 'green hill'? He dismissed it as only words. Now what to do about Sonia Fox. He had a growing mistrust of her for some unexplained reason, but he'd reached the point where he didn't know who to trust. The mantra 'Trust no one except yourself' came into his mind from somewhere.

His mood now somber and thoughtful, he strolled around the base of the tower as far as he could go before it became private property and then back to the steps, his only company some birds and the faint sound of passing traffic on the main road. Another walk to the fence and back and he'd made a decision.

DI Townshend answered the phone on its first ring and sounded surprised when Gregson said hello to him.

"I was just on the point of packing everything up and heading back to Peterborough," Townshend replied. "Where are you, or would you rather keep that to yourself?" Gregson explained where he was and what was happening. "So the elusive lady has re-appeared offering an explanation?"

"Yes. And I wondered if her explanation might help you about Tara Colman." Gregson still felt curiously guilty about the girl's death. "Can you get down here before tomorrow?"

"It's bit of a drive, but yes. Where am I going to meet you?" Gregson explained the instructions Sonia had given him. "OK, that shouldn't be a problem. Do I need back-up?"

"No, I'll be able to handle whatever happens." Gregson surprised himself with the comment, but not as much as he surprised the Detective Inspector who wondered where Gregson's unexpected confidence had come from.

CHAPTER FIFTEEN

The little church was boarded up, as he had been told it would be, derelict, redundant, unused and making a sad picture in the lovely landscape. Of all buildings that are no longer wanted, perhaps a church provides the most disconsolate image. Churches need to be used, to be loved, to be peopled. Gregson sighed, turned his back on the deserted building, found a seat and settled down to wait in the deserted and overgrown churchyard.

It was a certainly a lonely enough spot Sonia had chosen – the Cambrian mountains in the background and the reservoirs of the Elan Valley in the foreground and nothing moving apart from a solitary red kite in the sky. There was no wind and the water was still, reflecting the pale blue sky and its white puffy cotton wool looking clouds. He began to relax, whereas not half an hour ago in the Visitor Centre at the base of the reservoirs, drinking a cup of tea, he had felt the exact opposite – tense, nervous, wound up and much more. Some ferocious sounding dogs barking in the woods behind him shattered his peace for a few moments, but the tranquility of the place soon settled over him again.

It had been a difficult night's sleep for him, filled with dreams he didn't understand, dreams of killing and death where he seemed to be the instigator. Dreams normally eluded him as soon as the morning came, but these were different, vivid and unforgettable. He'd woken several times only to fall asleep again to a similar dream to the one that had woken him.

A car turned off the road on the far side of the reservoir, and headed towards him on the viaduct. Half expecting it to pull off into the parking area, and tensing at the thought, he was almost disappointed when it drove past and carried on up the hill. He settled down to wait again, the silence returning as the sound of the car receded and he continued to gaze out over the water, absorbing the stillness of everything around him.

"Mr Gregson," said a voice, startling him out of a reverie in which he was trying to comprehend what was so familiar about the phrase 'green hill.' "Nice to see you." With an effort of will power, Gregson forced himself not to turn around, but carried on gazing out over the view of the reservoir with its backdrop of mountains. He knew that voice, that velvety tone: Derek Townshend.

"Hello, Detective Inspector. Thank you for coming. This place is a bit out of the way." The other man sat down beside him on the seat.

"It does seem our paths are destined to cross every now and again," the detective said. "I certainly wasn't expecting a phone call from you. Has Mrs. Fox been in touch yet?"

"No, and I was hoping she wouldn't before you arrived. Are you armed, Detective Inspector?" The question came out of nowhere.

"No." The policeman looked serious. "Are you expecting trouble of some sort? I can call for armed backup."

"No, I don't think so." Gregson paused, uncertain as to whether or not to continue. "but I've been feeling all day that I'd feel happier with a gun of some sort," he said, still not looking away from the view. There was a much longer pause before the detective said anything.

"Do you have any experience with weapons, Mr Gregson?" Images from the previous night's dreams came into Gregson's mind. He'd certainly known what he was doing in them. He felt sure a gun would feel good in his hands.

"No," he replied.

"Well, you've told me we don't need backup so you can't consider Mrs. Fox dangerous. I don't understand." The policeman sounded terse, professional.

"Nor do I," said Gregson. For the first time since the policeman had arrived, Gregson turned to look at him, a half smile on his face. Townshend had spent his career studying faces, and there was something different about Gregson from the last time he'd seen him. There was a more determined set to his features, a look in his eyes that seemed to brook no argument. Yet it was still the same Malcolm Gregson speaking to him.

96

"There's a lot that I don't understand, Detective Inspector. Why would a woman like Sonia Fox turn to me for help? Why me? What help could a pen-pusher from the local town hall possibly give her?" Was that anger or confusion Townshend could hear in the other man's voice? He wasn't sure, but it was strange that Gregson had voiced the same question he'd been asking himself.

"Possibly because she had no one else to turn to she could trust after her brother was found dead. "It was a shot in the dark from Townshend, but it seemed to find its target. He was killed with Propofol, the same stuff used on Tara Colman and in a smaller dose, on you."

"Her brother? I didn't know she had a brother," Gregson replied.

"His name was Joseph," Townshend continued. Gregson shook his head,

"No. That was her husband's name. She was trying to get away from him." He went on to tell the policeman the details of the conversation he'd had with Sonia in the coffee shop.

"Look, Malcolm." He paused, remembering his professional position. "May I call you Malcolm? It seems so damned formal to carry on addressing you as Mr. Gregson, especially in a spot as lovely as this. Feel free to call me Derek. So much friendlier." Gregson nodded. "Joseph Fox was found dead yesterday and it appears he'd been dead for a few days, certainly before Sonia met you in Peterborough. Did you ever meet him? Do you remember him from school when you knew Sonia?"

Gregson thought about the question, and the more he thought about it, the less he seemed to be able to recall his schooldays. He'd had a real crush on Sonia, he was sure of that, but everything else was hazy, almost non-existent. He couldn't remember friends or teachers. Hell, he couldn't even remember what the school looked like!

"No, I can't remember. I don't think I ever met him." Gregson's voice was quiet, with a slight element of anxiety in it, Townshend thought. Was the man lying to him? One look at Gregson's face, anxious, worried, confused and angry, told him the answer was no. There was something wrong. Townshend said nothing and the two men sat quietly, both now gazing at the vista before them, and waiting. The arrival of a people carrier with tinted windows caught the attention of both men as it drove across the aqueduct and pulled into the picnic and parking area just below where they were sitting.

A man in casual clothes jumped out of the passenger door, followed by a young woman emerging from the driver's side of the vehicle. Both looked in their early thirties Townshend thought, and then as he watched they helped four other young people out of the carrier's side door and lowered an occupied wheelchair from the rear. Carers and a group of special needs adults he thought, turning his gaze and attention once more to the water and to the view. Gregson however, although seemingly lost in his own thoughts, kept on watching as the group turned towards a woodland walk. The young man said a few words to his companion and gestured to the church. She in turn gestured to the track ahead and moved on slowly with the group while he turned hurriedly on to the path towards the church and the waiting men. Gregson nudged Townshend.

"Someone's coming," he said, and had the policeman's attention immediately. They both watched the young man as he passed behind the hedge by the church, re-emerging on the path up to the churchyard. He visibly slowed as he noticed the two men watching him, and approached them very cautiously.

"Would one of you be Malcolm Gregson by any chance?" he asked. Gregson nodded and stood up. Townshend appeared to look disinterested. "My name's Doug West," he said nervously. "I was in the visitor centre with my friends," he continued, gesturing towards the group which had now disappeared into the trees, "and somebody came up and started talking to us." Townshend began to look a little more interested.

"A man or a woman?" he asked.

"Oh, a woman, a very attractive woman."

"Did she tell you her name?" As soon as the policeman asked, he realised it was a silly question. Names, like clothes and hair colour and styles were changeable to suit the occasion if you were that way inclined.

"Yes, Sonia, and she said to ask for you," looking towards Gregson. He sounded less nervous now, as if he was relieved to have found the two men reasonably approachable. "She told me you'd be waiting here, and asked me to give you this." He took a small package from his pocket and handed it over.

"Thank you," said Gregson, turning it over and over in his hands.

"Is it all right if I go now?" asked the young man. "I've got people to look after and ..." he paused. "I really don't want to get involved in anything." Gregson thanked him again, and the young man looked relieved to be allowed to walk away. Gregson waited until he was out of sight, following the track his companions had taken, before gingerly unwrapping the package. Inside was a short letter and a small plastic and metal device, the likes of which he hadn't seen before. He held it up to show Townshend.

"What is it?" he asked the detective.

"A data stick," replied Townshend "and we need a computer to find out what's on it, because whatever it is, someone wants us to know. I don't suppose you've got a lap-top in your car?"

"No. I don't even own one."

"Then we'll need to find a fair-sized police station and use one of their computers. Come on. Leave your car here. I'll get it picked up later."

"It's at the visitor centre. I walked up from there," Gregson explained.

"You walked? That's a good hike," Townshend said.

"The young girl on reception gave me the impression it was just a short stroll," Gregson said drily. "It would be good not to have to walk back."

"Then let's get moving." Townshend was intrigued. Could whatever was on this memory stick help him sort out what had happened to Tara Colman? Gregson's concern was more immediate. Why hadn't Sonia come herself? Why had she let him down again?

CHAPTER SIXTEEN

"REYNARD ENTERPRISES" flashed up on the screen when Townshend inserted the data stick into the computer.

"Joseph Fox's little business empire," the policeman commented, gesturing at the screen. "Hardly an imaginative name, is it?" He and Gregson were sitting in a small office in the main police station in Cardiff. Somehow, in his quiet and authorative way, and Gregson wasn't quite sure how, Townshend had managed to get them some privacy.

From Gregson's point of view, the trip from the Elan Valley to Cardiff, via Builth Wells and Rhayader, had been far from entertaining. For some reason which he didn't share, Townshend had decided to avoid smaller police stations and go directly to Cardiff. He'd driven to Builth Wells in a style remarkably unsuited to the albeit good valley roads and much more suited to the Welsh Rally. When the roads improved, Townshend had simply taken the opportunity to drive faster. Gregson had been almost delighted to get out of the policeman's car in the police station car park.

"So what is this little empire all about?" he asked, but before the policeman could answer they were interrupted by a young constable carrying two steaming hot cups of coffee.

"Thank you," Townshend said, and then to Gregson, "Making money, what else? He describes himself as an investment broker," he added.

"Meaning?"

"Meaning he plays with other people's money, supposedly working for commission."

"So he's loaded, then," Gregson said.

"Well off, certainly, but I wouldn't say loaded. From what I can gather, in the grand scheme of things, he's quite a small fish in a large pond playing with the big boys. But really, he's only peripheral to my enquiries."

"Is he any good at what he does?"

"Yes, but like everybody he makes mistakes, and when money's involved, any amount of money, making mistakes makes you enemies," Townshend said.

"And you think all this has something to do with Sonia?" Gregson was feeling out of his depth again, and trying to find some baseline.

"She is his sister and seems to be involved, so that is one angle, yes."

"One angle? You have others?"

"Yes." He changed tack without expanding. "Now, shall we see what it is that's so important on this memory stick?" Despite his curiosity about what the other angles might be, Gregson agreed. Townshend pressed the 'Enter' key on the keyboard and the screen sprang into life. The company logo disappeared and what appeared in its place seemed to Townshend to be a series of flashing images, punctuated by the word 'greenhill.' It made no sense. While waiting for something more useful, he took the opportunity to sip at his coffee, allowing his mind to wander, but keeping half an eye on the screen as the bewildering display of images continued. He took no notice of Gregson sat in the chair alongside him, assuming that he was also waiting. If he had looked across, he would have seen that the other man's gaze was riveted to the screen, his concentration totally on the images as if they meant something to him, blinking only when the word 'greenhill' flashed up occasionally. The images stopped almost as suddenly as they'd started and the 'REYNARD ENTERPRISES' logo returned.

"What the hell?" reacted Townshend angrily prodding at the 'Enter' key. Much to his satisfaction, he was rewarded with a display of folders and files. "Now, this is what we're looking for, something sensible," he said, leaning towards the screen. There was no reply and he glanced around. Gregson was sitting back in his chair, holding his head in his hands. "Are you okay?" Townshend asked him.

"Just feeling a bit faint. I'll be fine when I've drunk my coffee." He looked pale and haunted and not quite himself, but the policeman took him at his word. "Now what is there in these files

104

that's so important?" Gregson asked and the detective turned his attention back to the screen and began to display the contents of the first file. It was an invoice, as was the second and the third file. The detective turned to the folders where he found numerous images of bank statements and financial transactions, none of which Gregson could follow. The DI skipped quickly through page after page.

"If this is what I think it is, then this stuff's more important than I thought!" Townshend exclaimed.

"Is it?" Gregson asked, much less enthusiastically. "Why?" The DI looked away from the screen and directly at Gregson.

"It looks like proof that Joseph Fox has not only been acting illegally, he's been playing with the really big boys, well out of his league, and trying to swindle them as well. What an idiot. My colleagues at the Met will need to check this out thoroughly to be sure. It could give an indication as to why he was murdered and more importantly by who."

"That's all very well and good," said Gregson, feeling like a dog worrying at a bone, "but what has all this got to do with Sonia?" The only answer the detective could give him was an apologetic shake of the head.

"I don't know – yet, but it looks like Joseph has been up to no good with the Chinese government, or at least parts of it." A hand reached from behind both of them and jerked the memory stick from its slot.

"What you have here, gentlemen, if I may be so bold, or rather what I now have, is something of great interest, of national, possibly international interest, even." The voice that startled them both was recognised by Gregson. It was well-spoken and obviously well-educated. A voice that was used to being obeyed. Keith Blakeley. Gregson and Townshend both turned sharply. "Mr. Gregson, a pleasure to meet you again, and Detective Inspector Townshend, a pleasure to meet you." He did not extend his hand in greeting.

Keith Blakeley was feeling rather pleased with himself. After finding out about the meeting at Elan from listening in to Gregson's phone calls the previous day, he'd put in place plans to have the men watched and if necessary, followed, although it had been Sonia he really wanted to talk to. He was almost as annoyed as Gregson that she hadn't turned up, but at least he now had the evidence he so dearly wanted. He was just about to slip it into his pocket when Gregson grabbed his wrist, standing and pushing his chair to the floor.

"Are you going to tell me why you're so interested in this and why you've been following me?" His voice sounded harsh and menacing, something Blakeley didn't recall from their meeting in Canterbury. Gregson's grip was strong, stronger than Blakeley might have expected, but he calmly prised his wrist free of the man's grip.

"No to the first," he said, "and as for the second, I told you in Canterbury. I want Sonia Fox, and you looked like the best way of

106

finding her. Shame I was wrong about that, but at least I've now got this." He waved the data stick and this time did slip it into his pocket.

"That is evidence in a police investigation," said the DI also rising to face Blakeley.

"No, it isn't, Detective Inspector. As far as you're concerned, this piece of evidence, as you put it, is history, as is your investigation."

"What do you mean, 'history'?"

"As of now, your investigation has been closed down and the matter moved out of your jurisdiction. It no longer concerns you, Detective Inspector." Blakeley's matter of fact tone seemed to be annoying the normally calm policeman.

"Just who the hell are you to be telling me that? And come to that how did you get access to these offices?" Blakeley smiled and reached inside his jacket, and drew out a small wallet containing an ID card.

"Satisfied, Detective Inspector?"

"No, but it seems I have no choice, sir." He emphasised the last word so much that it sounded almost like an insult. Blakeley took no notice of the tone, simply smiled and walked out of the office without a word, leaving Gregson and Townshend looking at each other. It would have been difficult for an onlooker to tell which of them was the more angry. Both had far too many questions which now looked as if they would never be answered.

"So that was the man you talked to in Canterbury?" It was the detective who broke the silence.

"Yes, Keith Blakeley. Just who the hell is he and how did he do what he just did?"

"Commander Keith Blakeley, to give him his full title and he works for British Intelligence. That should tell you everything." Townshend was right and there didn't seem to be anything Gregson could say. Both men fell silent again.

"Is there somewhere I can get some fresh air? I'm still feeling muggy-headed." Gregson said after a long pause. He hadn't felt right since sitting in front of the computer screen. The detective led him outside to the enclosed car park.

"Will you be okay out here while I make some phone calls?" he asked. Gregson nodded, and Townshend showed him a small buzzer set in the wall. "When you're ready, press that and ask for me. Then we'll see about getting you back to your bed and breakfast."

Once alone, Gregson paced around the car park, confused and increasingly angry. Some of the images on the computer screen had seemed so familiar, others too similar to his dreams to be comfortable and others unbelievable, but still he'd been unable to take his eyes off them. He actually felt as if his mind was unraveling, but why? He put his hands in his pockets and touched the note that he'd stuffed there at the Elan Valley. The note from Sonia, or at least that's what he assumed. He hadn't read it yet. He unfolded it as he walked.

"My dearest Malcolm'

I'm so sorry I couldn't give this to you in person, but there are reasons for that I can't go into just yet. You need an explanation, my darling. No, you deserve an explanation. Things might be becoming a little clearer to you as the days go by, or at least I hope so. To help, there is something on the memory stick for you, should you get to see it. The rest is of no consequence to you. Please believe me when I say I never meant any of this to happen or to drag you into it, but there was no one else I could trust enough.

To past memories,

Sonia"

CHAPTER SEVENTEEN

Gregson woke up feeling exhausted and not in the least refreshed. Sunlight was streaming in through the curtained bedroom window and it took him a few moments to realise where he was. Until he got his bearings and his thoughts in order, he lay looking at the partially beamed ceiling. It was a habit he'd grown into over the years, waking an hour or so before his alarm went off. The early morning had become his own time, when he had no responsibility to get anything done and no need to be anywhere. He could just be alone with his thoughts, but this particular morning that was the last thing he wanted.

It had been a profound shock to Gregson the day before when he'd realised he had no memories of his schooldays, but during the course of the evening and the largely sleepless night he'd just endured, it had grown much, much worse. The final blow had been that prior to his recent memories of just a few years, there was nothing. No childhood memories, no memories of parents or home, none of girlfriends, except, strangely, his infatuation with Sonia, none of university, or even if he went. Did he go, or didn't he? He couldn't even remember learning how to drive, but he could certainly do that. It was almost frightening.

And then there was Amanda, his wife. He'd been married to her, but he couldn't think of where they'd first met, their first date. He couldn't even remember his wedding day, but he'd seen photos of that. None of it made sense. He dragged himself out of bed and made himself a coffee with the small guest kettle to calm his nerves, then crossed to the window, where he pulled the curtain back, opening the window wide and shivering a little after the warmth of the blankets he'd just left. He watched transfixed while various shades of grey took on their different colours as the world presented itself to a brand new day. There was always something special about watching the day begin, something fresh about the air and a gentle feeling of hope hanging over everything.

Could it have been an accident of some sort? Did he lose his memory in a car crash or something like that? He certainly had scars on his body which he couldn't remember getting and up until this whole sorry mess had started he'd been taking tablets of some sort. His doctor. He could see his doctor to see if the man could shed some light on anything. But was it a man, or was it a woman? With a sinking feeling, he realised he didn't remember ever seeing a doctor, let alone remembering who or where.

Thinking of scars caused his mind to jump. What about those oh so familiar dreams? Vivid and violent as they were, if they were even half real, it would explain some of the scars; but the person in the dreams wasn't him, couldn't possibly be him. That man's life wasn't his; Gregson was nothing more or less than a pen-pusher in a council planning office. His mind wasn't going to let go of this train of thought and leapt to the images that had been on the memory stick, images Sonia had said were there for him to see. He'd known those faces, been to those places. He knew he had. And the words 'green hill'. What the hell was that all about? He knew it was important, but its meaning seemed just out of grasp, like seeing something out of the corner of your eye and turning to find it wasn't there.

He'd come to the final puzzle: Sonia's note. He made another coffee and retrieved the note from his jacket before returning to his seat at the window. It didn't make sense, any more than anything else did. She'd called him 'my dearest' and 'my darling' and signed off 'to past memories' and he simply didn't understand. And there was the phrase 'things might be becoming clearer to you as the days go by'. Well they certainly weren't, but what was there to become clearer?

A car passing down the lane far too fast jerked him away from the reverie he'd been on the verge of slipping into. It screeched sideways at the bottom of the narrow road, blocking it completely. Minutes passed and nothing happened. There was no movement, and no one climbed out. The car just sat there and his thoughts settled again. The slow monotonous ticking of the grandfather clock in the hallway outside his room helped relax his thinking, settled him into a rhythm of breathing and a peaceful calm he rather liked. After all, this place was a retreat, a place to get away from it all.

He was gazing almost absently out of the window when the car door opened and a woman climbed out. As she looked up at the bed and breakfast, he instinctively pulled back from the window and from her view, for some reason he couldn't explain not wanting to be seen. He shook his head. She was probably nothing more than a prospective guest for the bed and breakfast and for the McNally's, although there was something familiar about her, something he couldn't quite place. He leaned forward a little and watched her walk across the road and up to the gate of the house. He looked more closely. It was a face from the images he'd seen the day before, one of the images that kept repeating and he knew without thinking that she represented danger.

He'd finished dressing hurriedly by the time the front door bell rang and softly opened the door of his room and crept out onto the landing. Greetings were being exchanged, but when the hallway below came into view, he was surprised to see both Gwen and Phil McNally there. The visitor's voice was muffled when she spoke, but Phil McNally's came up to him clearly.

"I'm so sorry miss, but we really don't have any rooms available. We're re-decorating after a serious leak. If you'd like to pop back down into the town, the girls in the Tourist Office should be able to help you. The office is in the tower in the market place." He sounded polite but firm. His wife was standing behind him slightly to one side, and Gregson could see she was holding something in her right hand, hidden from the visitor's view, but he couldn't quite make out what. A few more words were exchanged, with Phil McNally sounding even more firm, and then Gregson heard two soft 'crump' sounds quickly following each other. As

113

Phil and Gwen McNally both fell to the floor, Gregson recognised the noise immediately – a silenced pistol. A small pool of blood was already forming under Gwen McNally's head as the visitor stepped over their bodies, and as he pulled quickly back, Gregson caught a glimpse of what Gwen McNally had been holding, sending his mind reeling. Lying on the floor close to her body was another pistol.

Back in his room, he turned directly towards the window, already wide open and dropped to the porch roof below, then down to the ground, landing easily on his feet. Moving quickly with an instinct that came from who knows where, he moved away, heading for the rear of the house. Those same instincts told him he needed a weapon, and the only one available was lying in the hallway of the bed and breakfast. Ignoring the question of why Gwen McNally might have a gun, he concentrated instead on how he was going to get hold of it for himself.

From outside the conservatory, and looking through the dining room to the open door of the hallway, he saw the woman start up the stairs, stepping once more over Gwen McNally's body, and thankfully ignoring the weapon. Without any hesitation, and praying that Phil McNally had been true to his habit of going into the garden through the conservatory for an early morning cigarette so that it was unlocked, he grasped the door handle and turned it. It opened silently, much to his relief, and he re-entered the house, his steps quiet on the thick carpet. Reaching the hall,

114

he crouched down in the doorway and stretched out his hand for the gun.

"Leave it alone, Mr. Gregson," said a voice from the landing, a voice he recognised straight away: the woman from Canterbury. Hoping for surprise to be on his side, he dived down the hallway towards the kitchen door, where he couldn't be seen from upstairs, grabbing up the gun as he rolled. He didn't hear the soft 'crump' of the pistol but he certainly felt the pain in his trailing leg as the bullet hit home. His mind registered that it was a pain he somehow felt he'd experienced before, but a yell still escaped his lips as he fell into the kitchen, scrabbling on the floor to get to the back door before she came downstairs to finish him off. He'd almost reached it when the room began to swim before his eyes, and he slipped gently into unconsciousness.

CHAPTER EIGHTEEN

Sterile, clinical, glaring white was all he could see. Everything white, not that there was much in the room apart from the bed he was lying in. Walls, ceiling, floor and door, all white, unrelenting, unrelieved white. There was no window and the single light, harsh and bright, hanging from the ceiling directly above the bed, was unshaded. He couldn't close his eyes in an attempt to sleep, but sleep wouldn't come anyway, kept at bay by thoughts tumbling over themselves in his mind. Where was he? What was happening to him, or rather, what was being done to him?

The fear of the unknown, of simply not knowing, gripped him, almost sending him into a panic. He opened his eyes again. Even the harsh white was better than the growing panic. His stomach rumbled. He felt hungry and thirsty. When did he eat or drink last? He didn't know. As if on cue, the door to the cell opened. Why did he think of it as that, he wondered. Why a cell and not a room? A nurse appeared at his bedside with a tray and his hopes rose, only to fall just as quickly. No food, just tablets, a lot of tablets, and water.

He tried to sit up, but couldn't move. Nothing would move, not his arms or his legs, nor his hands or feet. It was too much of an effort to try; he was just too tired, too weak. He couldn't even raise his head. The nurse popped the tablets into his mouth, one at a time, each one accompanied by a sip of water. When she

116

stopped, he tried to speak, to tell her he was hungry, but no words came, no sound came out of his mouth. Without even so much as a smile, she turned and left the room, closing the door behind her, leaving him alone in his white world. He slept.

When he woke, he had no idea of how long he'd slept. There was no way to tell, no reference point. There was no clock and he didn't know what time it was, or even if it was day or night. He had no idea of how long he'd been in this room or when he'd been brought here. This room was all he knew, there was nothing before; no memories of any sort, just this awful white room. The door opened again. This time it was two people that entered, a man and a woman, both dressed in white from head to toe.

"Hello, Mr. Gregson, or can I call you Malcolm?" the man said with forced cheerfulness. "How are you today?" The woman said nothing, just looking down at him. She seemed to be holding something in her hand.

"That's not my name," he said from the bed. No sound came out of his mouth despite the words being loud and clear in his mind. "That's not my name," he tried again, still making no sound. The woman produced a syringe. Frustrated and fearful, he tried to pull away from the needle, but couldn't move.

CHAPTER NINETEEN

"That's not my name," Gregson said groggily as he came round, blinking his eyes in the bright sunlight pouring into the McNally's kitchen.

"What's not your name?" asked the woman sitting across the kitchen table from him. He really didn't like her voice. Gwen McNally's pistol was on the table in front of her.

"What?" he asked in return. "I think I must have been dreaming," he continued. He tried to stretch his arms and found he was tied to a chair. His legs seemed to be free, however.

"Just to stop you falling off, Mr. Gregson. Wouldn't want you hurt now, would I?"

"After you've just shot me?" He tested the ropes. They were tight.

"Only with a tranquillizer, Mr. Gregson. You've had it before, you know." She laughed. "Any more of this Propofol stuff and you'll be turning into an addict." She noticed him still testing the ropes that bound him. "Don't struggle. I'll let you go when I'm ready. It's not you I'm after, although you are of use to me."

"You won't find what you're after now. It's in safe hands," Gregson said.

"Oh?" To his surprise, she didn't sound too interested. "So who does have it?"

"The British Government," said Gregson and stopped. He still felt groggy from the tranquillizer and it had just occurred to him

118

that despite what she'd said about letting him go, he'd witnessed her murdering two people.

"Never mind," she said smiling rather coldly. "I'd much rather you told me where Sonia Fox is."

"Sonia? Why?"

"Because I've got unfinished business with the bitch!" A flash of anger crossed her face. Wondering just what that business might be, Gregson flexed his left leg, where he'd been caught by the tranquillizer. It felt a little stiff, but otherwise fine. He looked at the woman.

"Sounds serious," he said and was rewarded with another flash of anger in her eyes. He pushed his chair back from the table and she half rose at his movement, but then he suddenly slumped forward as if he'd passed out again. The woman rose completely this time and came round the table towards him. When she was close enough to him, he tipped the chair over to his left and swung his right leg high and hard against her head, his shoe catching her under the ear by her jaw. She fell to the floor as if pole-axed, an astonished look on her face.

So far so good, thought Gregson, surprised at his own actions, but the problem now was how to get free before she recovered, which might not be long. There was still washing up from last night to be dried in the drainer, he'd noticed that, so hopefully there'd be a knife amongst it sharp enough to cut the ropes. He kicked out a few times without any success in dislodging it and gave up on the idea. It took a tremendous amount of effort, but he managed to pull himself and the chair upright once more and he re-thought the situation. It wasn't thick rope, so could he find somewhere sharpish he could rub it against and hopefully work through it? The jutting corner of the utility room wall would do if he could get the chair close enough.

It was harder work than he thought it would be, and the ropes were only just beginning to part, freeing him from the chair when the woman showed the first signs of reviving. He pulled hard against the ropes and kept rubbing his hands up and down the wall until finally they came free and then took a few short moments to get the blood flowing again. He took up the pistol from the table and checked it was loaded, not giving any thought as to how he knew how to do it, just doing it. He was sitting at the table holding the pistol in both hands and pointing it at the woman when her eyes opened.

"Do you know how to use that?" she asked calmly.

"I don't know. Do you want to find out?" He hoped he sounded more confident than he was feeling, but he had to admit, the weapon, small though it was, felt very comfortable in his hand. She shook her head, smiling.

"No. I don't think we'll put it to the test, Mr. Gregson. It looks as if you have the upper hand at the moment." She paused. "I may have underestimated you, usually a fatal mistake in my line of work." She tried to settle herself more comfortably, sitting on the floor against a kitchen cupboard. A trickle of blood was running down her neck and she rubbed her jaw with a grimace.

"I've got some questions," he said, "and I'm hoping you can give me some answers." She nodded. "First, where's your gun?" She glanced down.

"In my pocket," she replied.

"Take it out carefully and toss it into the hallway, as far as you can." She did as she was told. "Now, why have you been following me?" he asked.

"I wanted you to lead me to Sonia Fox."

"Because of what she had?"

"Partly. And as I told you we have unfinished business."

"And you want to finish that business?"

"Oh yes, and I fully intend to." She sounded confident.

"What is it?" Gregson asked.

"The unfinished business?" It was Gregson's turn to nod. "I'm going to kill her." He was stunned. It was said in such a matter of fact way, almost as if she was talking about going shopping.

"Kill her? Why?"

"She not only slept with someone I cared for, she killed him afterwards."

"She did what? She killed somebody? Sonia?" He was incredulous. It dawned on him suddenly that he knew very, very little about the woman he thought he'd known at school. He knew his thoughts must be showing on his face when she spoke.

"You know nothing about her do you?" She didn't let him answer. "She's a killer, Mr. Gregson, like me." She started to push home what she thought was an advantage. "She calls herself a government officer, working for the British government, but that's what she does for them. She kills." Gregson was stunned.

"And what about you? Who do you work for?"

"Whoever pays me the most. It's that simple. But with her, it's personal."

"How am I involved in this?"

"I don't know. I really don't know." She sounded almost apologetic. "I think she's using you in some way. When you see her, ask her, but you won't get a straight answer from the scheming bitch." She began to get up from the floor, still keeping her eye on him. "It's time we stopped this foolishness, don't you think?" she said. "And I really don't think you're going to use that thing on me, are you?" As she rose, however, she noticed that he moved the pistol to follow her, and realised the weapon was pointing at her forehead. The assassin's shot, a single shot kill. More than anything, it surprised her. Did he know what he was doing, or was it just coincidence? Gregson just sat there watching her, saying nothing. He didn't know what to do, apart from possibly call the police about the McNallys.

"Why did you kill them?" he asked.

"Who?"

"The McNallys. Why did you kill them?"

"They were stopping me getting to you, and they were dangerous. She was holding a gun, you know."

"Dangerous? How?" He'd been about to say that they were a harmless couple, but he had to admit she was right about that gun. He didn't understand that.

"Mr. Gregson, this is what is known as a 'safe house'," she said, "and they were its caretakers." Gregson suddenly felt as if his pot of unanswered questions had reached the point of overflowing. She must have noticed. "No, Mr. Gregson, I don't know what you're doing in a safe house either."

"But I've been coming here for years," he said. It didn't escape her notice that the gun wavered a little in his hands. Was this a chance? After all, she thought, the man was an out and out amateur, especially compared to her.

"What's your name?" he suddenly asked. The question came at her out of the blue.

"Why would you want to know that?" She was suddenly suspicious; it was second nature to her.

"I'm just interested, and I'm the one holding the gun," he replied. "And I might want to pass on your regards to Sonia Fox." She smiled. After holding a gun on her, there was no way this man was going to be around long enough to ever see Sonia Fox again. She still hesitated, however, considering lying to him, but decided against it.

"Cara Bingham." Time froze for Gregson. Images flashed across his mind, the images he'd seen yesterday, the images Sonia had told him in the note were for him. Amongst them were pictures of this woman, Cara Bingham, and attached to each of them was a subliminal message for his eyes only. The message transferred itself to his fingers without any conscious thought on his part. He pulled the trigger.

CHAPTER TWENTY

His bemused fascination with the single bloody hole in Cara Bingham's forehead and the surprised stunned look on her face soon gave way to the unforgiving twin sisters of remorse and regret. He'd taken a life, coldly, calmly and unfeelingly. One second she was a living breathing woman, and the next, nothing more than a lump of flesh and bone. And he was responsible. The negative thoughts spiralled. Who was he to take on the authority to end another person's life, to judge whether or not she was worthy of living? He dropped the gun, closed his eyes and held his head in his hands. He'd had no right to do what he'd just done and what was worse, had no idea of why he'd done it.

His mind was spinning out of control. He wouldn't do this again, couldn't do this again. It was wrong to set yourself up as an executioner. They couldn't make him do it again, he thought, without wondering who 'they' might be. He wouldn't do it. He opened his eyes and the splashes of blood on the kitchen wall from the exit wound in Cara Bingham's head jolted him back into full consciousness and focussed his thoughts.

"Oh, my God," he whispered to himself. He looked down at the gun and then over once more at Cara Bingham's body. Then he turned and looked at the bodies of the McNallys. Christ, what a mess, he thought, and I'm in the middle of it. He had to do something, but what? What was there that he could possibly do to sort this out? Ring it in, prompted a voice from somewhere in his mind. Job done. Ring it in. More mind tricks. He was suffering from them more and more with each passing day. Who could he ring? Not the police, not with three dead bodies and that also ruled out Derek Townshend. Then it came to him. Keith Blakeley. That was the answer. He was something high up in the government, so he should be able to sort things out or at least know someone who could. He would still have Sonia's mobile phone, and Gregson had the number.

When it rang, Sonia Fox's mobile was sitting in the bottom drawer of Keith Blakeley's desk and it took him a few moments to find it and then a little longer while he checked the display to see who was calling.

"Hello, Mr. Gregson, or can I call you Malcolm?" he said. At the other end in Talgarth, Gregson's mind somersaulted again. He'd heard those exact words when he was unconscious and dreaming earlier and his mind reacted in the same way as it had done then, but this time out loud.

"That's not my name," he replied, confusing Keith Blakeley, who recognised the voice. It wasn't one he'd expected to hear again. He was quite sharp in his response.

"Well, if Malcolm Gregson isn't your name, what is?"

"Martin Grant." The reply was immediate and instinctive, and even though Gregson didn't know where it came from, he knew it was true.

"Well, Martin or Malcolm or whatever you've decided to call yourself, what can I do for you?"

"I have a problem relating to Sonia Fox," Gregson said and Keith Blakeley was suddenly very, very interested.

"In what way?" he asked. He still wanted to talk to Sonia Fox.

"Someone wants to kill her," Gregson said, then rephrased it slightly. "No, someone was trying to kill her." There was a long pause from Blakeley.

"Do you know who?"

"Yes, a woman named Cara Bingham, the same woman who followed me to Canterbury."

"Where is she now?" There was a bit more urgency in this question.

"Dead," Gregson said, trying to keep his voice as calm as possible.

"Dead? How do you know?"

"I killed her." This time there was an even longer pause before Keith Blakeley said anything.

"Where are you, Malcolm?" Gregson explained about the bed and breakfast in Talgarth, how Cara had killed the McNallys and everything that had happened after.

"She said something about it being a safe house," he added. "The bed and breakfast, that is."

"Who did? Sonia Fox?"

"No, Cara Bingham, just before I shot her."

"Malcolm, I must ask you this. Why did you kill her?" Blakeley was now proceeding as gently as he could. He'd recognised from his voice that Malcolm Gregson was a man on the edge of cracking up.

"I don't know. I just knew I had to. It was when she told me her name," was Gregson's reply. Keith Blakeley pushed a button on his desk to summon his departmental deputy. The whole situation, and Malcolm Gregson in particular, needed careful handling. It seemed to have erupted from nowhere. Three dead bodies in a safe house on the Welsh borders, along with an unpredictable man who could best be described as being in an 'unstable emotional state.'

"Malcolm, for your own sake, you need to stay calm and for the time being, stay where you are. We need to get

you out of there, but apart from your personal belongings, you need to leave everything exactly as it is. Don't touch anything. Do you understand?"

"Yes."

"I'll arrange for a car to be there as soon as possible to pick you up and take you somewhere where you'll be safe. We'll send a clean-up team and handle everything else. There will be no repercussions on you. Do you understand?" he asked again.

"Yes, perfectly," said Gregson. "And thank you," he added as he disconnected the call. Placing the phone on the kitchen table, he picked the gun up and slipped it into his pocket, smiling. A quick search of the kitchen produced a small box of ammunition for the weapon, and painkillers antiseptic and a bandage for the wound caused by the tranquillizer dart which was proving more painful as the tranquillizer itself wore off. With a last almost sad look at Cara Bingham's body he slipped out of the back door into the garden and then into the lane beyond. Something in the tone of Keith Blakeley's voice during the call had alarmed his new found instincts and triggered a reaction. When the car arrived, Malcolm Gregson had no intention of still being anywhere near the bed and breakfast to be 'picked up and taken somewhere safe.'

CHAPTER TWENTY-ONE

There was more to Keith Blakeley's department than met the eye, rather like an iceberg or a paddling duck and Blakeley himself, a relative newcomer – he'd only been in post for four years – still wasn't truly aware of the depths of everything that went on. The department and particularly Blakeley's able deputy Colin Lennon, seemed to have its fingers in a lot of pies, some of them more unsavoury than others.

Colin Lennon, a tall, thin and unhealthy looking man in his late thirties, his hair greying prematurely, sat on the other side of Keith Blakeley's desk, calmly listening to his superior's description of Malcolm Gregson's unexpected phone call. Blakeley had already issued his instructions, which Lennon had immediately passed on for action. The deputy's eyebrows had risen a little at Blakeley's mention of a safe house, but for the time being, he said nothing. Lennon was, in Blakeley's opinion, the fount of all knowledge and behind the man's placid and unruffled expression, all sorts of alarm bells were ringing and had been since Blakeley had mentioned two names – Martin Grant and Cara Bingham. The second had especially alarmed him. Lennon had been recruited directly from university and was a career 'spook', his entire working life of twenty two years – so far – had been spent in intelligence circles, and he knew that name, knew it all too well.

"How did this man Gregson know it was Cara Bingham, sir?" he asked during a short pause.

"I presume she told him," Blakeley replied. "I can't believe he'd ask her," he added drily. Lennon considered that before continuing.

"She must have felt confident to tell him her real name, sir" he said.

"Confident, Colin? Why?"

"Confident that she'd be able to handle the situation and that she'd be the one to walk away, sir," Lennon said. "If she thought that this man Gregson might be the one to survive their meeting, she would have lied, I'm sure."

"Sure, Colin? You seem to know a lot about the woman."

"I do, sir. She's a killer, one of the best. There's no other way of describing her. Hires herself out to whoever will pay her the most."

"And Malcolm Gregson or Martin Grant or whoever he is, has killed her." It was a statement that Keith Blakeley, having met Gregson, found hard to believe.

"So it seems, sir," Lennon said, and not for the first time since taking over the department, Blakeley had the feeling his deputy was keeping something from him. "There is one thing that worries me, sir," Lennon continued.

"Yes, Colin?"

"How would Cara Bingham know that the bed and breakfast in Talgarth was a safe house? And why was this man Gregson staying there? I'll have to get someone onto this. It seems like a breach of security."

"Yes, do that, Colin, and then can you get hold of some files for me?"

"Which ones, sir?" asked Lennon, knowing perfectly well what was coming, but showing no reaction.

"Sonia Fox and Cara Bingham, and see if you can get hold of anything on this name Martin Grant, will you?"

"Of course, sir," Lennon said, and yet again Blakeley sensed something was being held back from him. When his deputy left the office, Blakeley turned to his window, gazing out at the London skyline.

Blakeley was still facing the window when Lennon returned, knocking politely on the door before entering the office, but his mood was far different.

"He wasn't there," he snapped at Lennon, turning his chair back to face him.

"Who, sir?"

"Gregson or Grant or whatever his damned name is." Lennon wasn't really surprised. "The clean up team found the place empty, apart from the dead bodies, of course. They suspect he's armed as well. They couldn't find a second weapon, only Bingham's." Blakeley drew a breath. "He sounded unpredictable on the phone, Colin, and now he's got a gun. He has to be found."

"Yes, sir. We'll make it a priority. I would imagine he's scared, sir," he said.

"Scared or not, Colin, he could be dangerous."

"Dangerous to whom, sir?" asked Lennon.

"I don't know, Colin. I don't know why Sonia Fox involved him in the first place and it's not knowing that worries me. Now did you get those files I asked for? They might hold some answers."

"Yes, sir," replied Lennon, placing the files on Blakeley's desk. "I took the liberty of adding our file on Malcolm Gregson as well, sir."

"We have one?"

"Surprisingly, yes, sir." Motioning his deputy to take a seat, Blakeley settled in for some reading. Cara Bingham's file was by far the thickest, but he gave it only a cursory glance, seeing enough to think that the world was probably a better place without her, while at the same time wondering why nothing had been done to remove her much earlier. The information contained in the file was also enough to make Blakeley wonder how on earth Malcolm Gregson had been the person to eliminate her. He said as much to Lennon.

"It's a good question, sir," was the non-committal reply.

"Why was she never dealt with before?" Blakeley asked. This time he received a much more definite answer, but not the one he was expecting.

"She was of use to us, sir, on several occasions." Blakeley interrupted before Lennon could continue.

"Colin, are you telling me this department paid for her services?"

"No, sir. Not at all. It just happened that on certain occasions we were aware that her target was someone we would be just as happy to have removed as her clients. It was convenient, with no possible comeback to ourselves."

"So earlier, you recognised her name immediately?"

"Yes, sir."

"Mmmm," was the only comment Blakeley made and resumed reading. Colin Lennon ignored the disapproval in his superior's tone.

"I think, sir, that you might find Sonia Fox's file of some interest." Blakeley looked up again but found no expression on his deputy's face. Closing Cara Bingham's file, he took up the thinner one of Sonia Fox.

Educated at Bristol University, with a first class degree in modern European history, she was apparently a keen and talented sportswoman and had been recruited into the murky world of intelligence shortly before leaving Bristol. A psychological report described her as 'cold and calculating, able to completely dissociate herself from feelings of guilt or remorse.' Blakeley looked up again at Lennon.

"Have you read this file, Colin?" he asked.

"No, sir, but I am aware of some of the things it might contain, as well as some of the things it might not." After another sharp glance at his deputy, Blakeley continued reading. Then something occurred to him, and he turned back to the pages dealing with her education. After a quick glance, he looked up again at Colin Lennon.

"Is this right about where Sonia Fox went to school?" he asked.

"All of the data in the files is meticulously checked, sir, so I would imagine it is. Why do you ask?" Blakeley didn't reply immediately, but instead asked another question.

"Is there anything in Malcolm Gregson's file about where he went to school?"

"His file is very sparse, sir, but I will look." It didn't take him long to come up with the answer. "A secondary school in Peterborough, sir. Educated to GCSE level, but no further."

"Definitely Peterborough, Colin?"

"Yes, sir. Is it important?"

"When I met Malcolm Gregson in Canterbury, he told me that he and Sonia knew each other at school, yet his file says he went to school in Peterborough and her file says she attended a school in Bristol."

"I see, sir. They couldn't have known each other at school, so was he lying?"

"If he was, Colin, how much else of what he's said can we believe?" Blakeley returned briefly to Sonia Fox's file before asking another question.

"Personnel operative, Colin? I take it that covers up what she actually does?" His deputy nodded.

"A departmental euphemism, sir." Blakeley snorted. It didn't take much of a leap of his imagination to work out what it meant.

"That would explain some of the gaps in her file." Lennon nodded. "Is she good at her job, Colin?"

"Oh yes, sir. One of the best, absolutely ruthless." Blakeley snorted again. Two women, one alive, one dead, both seemingly highly trained killers, both involved in an apparent plan to subvert the British economy. Throw in a loose cannon in the shape of this Malcolm Gregson, armed and sounding like he was on the edge of a breakdown and who may be playing his own game, and things were becoming a little too complex. He looked at the last entry in Sonia Fox's file.

"What's this entry all about, Colin? Project Officer for Operation Greenhill?"

"I'm not really sure, sir. The files on Greenhill are too highly classified for access, even at your level, but there were rumours around the department a few years ago that it had something to do with experimental interrogation and brain washing techniques. Other than that, I couldn't really say, sir." Lennon sounded apologetic about this gap in his knowledge. Blakeley closed the file on Sonia Fox thoughtfully, and selected the next one: Martin Grant.

"And just who is Martin Grant, Colin?" he asked.

CHAPTER TWENTY-TWO

It was a question Malcolm Gregson was also asking himself. Who is Martin Grant? Since saying the name during the phone call to Keith Blakeley, he just couldn't shake it out of his mind, clashing for attention with the phrase 'green hill.' He was now unable to shake off the deep conviction that both of them were somehow very important to him. There didn't seem to be any pattern or connection to anything that had happened to him in the last few days and the long drive from the bed and breakfast at Talgarth back to Peterborough was giving him far too much time to think. The M4 from where he'd joined it at Newport to where he turned off onto the M25 was interminable, although crossing the second Severn Bridge was an enjoyable experience.

From the bed and breakfast, he'd gone straight to Cara Bingham's car, relieved to find the keys were still in the ignition. He'd thought as he approached it that he might have to return to the kitchen to look for them. He felt no remorse about taking the car, nor did he about checking the dead woman's handbag for money, as his own funds were running short. Luckily, the car also had nearly a full tank of petrol.

Driving out of Talgarth and taking the Abergavenny road, it had taken him a few minutes to decide where to go. He had no home anymore, so he was free to go anywhere he chose, but the practical, sensible side of him had told to return to Peterborough and at least sort out the insurance on his house to give him some money. He was well on his way as Keith Blakeley and Colin Lennon were having their discussion in a London office, but it was hours after that before he pulled into a hotel car park on the outskirts of Peterborough, physically tired from the drive and also mentally exhausted, his mind having been tying itself in knots. Although he couldn't remember why he'd been seeing her, he remembered a psychologist telling him that our minds never stop working, with thoughts constantly tumbling over themselves; the best we can do is try to control them. He was failing miserably.

After booking himself in at reception he went to his room. His leg was beginning to throb again with pain and a hospital was out of the question. He took some more painkillers before taking himself off for a walk, to refresh his mind after the long drive. The hotel overlooked a rowing lake, and he resolved to walk around it before eating, but found he couldn't. The pain in his leg prevented him walking that far. But even the short walk refreshed him and gave him an appetite. What it didn't do was erase the image of Cara Bingham's inert body in the McNally's kitchen and the inescapable fact that he'd shot her in cold blood. The image haunted him all through a sleepless night.

He had an early breakfast alone in the hotel restaurant sat by a window. Even at that hour the rowing lake, misty in the morning light, was busy with rowers training. There was a chill in the air when he took his coffee out onto the verandah to watch them. Tired though he was, there were things he had to do, and top of that list was the insurance company. He'd always done his business in their office in town, preferring to deal with someone face to face over a counter than some disembodied voice on the telephone.

He reached the office just as they were opening, after walking into town along the river path. When he explained why he was there, the young woman behind the counter asked him to wait for a few moments, and then he was ushered through to the manager's office.

"Mr. Gregson, I believe you're here about 19 Milton Avenue. A sad business. I believe the police suspect arson?" Gregson nodded. "We can process your claims for contents through the office today, while you're here. Do you have the crime number they've assigned?"

"Crime number?" Gregson asked.

"Yes. The police will have assigned a crime number as the fire wasn't accidental. We'll need that to put the claim through, but if you don't have it at the moment, we can partially complete the claim and finish it off when you do have it. Shall we go ahead with what we can do?" Gregson nodded, adding that he would be back soon with the necessary number, but then a question occurred to him.

"Did you say 'contents'?" he asked.

"Yes, Mr. Gregson."

"What about the house itself?" Gregson asked.

"The house? I don't understand."

"Yes, a claim against the building being destroyed."

"That claim has already been dealt with for the building's owner, Mr. Gregson," the manager said. "The only claim outstanding is for the contents."

"But I owned it," Gregson said.

"Apparently not."

"Well I certainly bloody lived there. If I didn't own it, who did?"

"I'm not sure if I'm at liberty to say, Mr. Gregson"

"It can't be a state secret, can it?" Gregson asked, irritation showing in his voice. Something about him encouraged the man sitting across the desk to do as he was asked. He pressed a few keys on the computer on his desk.

"Greenhill Management, Mr. Gregson. Did you not know?" Gregson didn't answer the question, indeed didn't say anything. He rose and left the office in a daze of confusion, the manager calling after him. "Did you want to proceed with the claim, Mr. Gregson?" Gregson ignored him, walking down the street until he found a bench he could sit on and think.

He stayed there for some time lost in thought, before going into a coffee shop and buying himself a takeaway coffee. He needed a library, and access to a computer. 'Greenhill Management' had thrown him almost as much as finding out he didn't own his house. He'd just assumed he did. Was it just a coincidence, those words 'green hill'? Why did they keep popping up? He wished to God he knew for sure, because he had a strong feeling it was very important to him. An internet search might help. He finished his drink.

With a little help from a friendly librarian, he was soon up and running on one of their public computers. Typing in 'green hill' produced more results than he'd expected, millions of them, and for a few moments he just sat looking at the screen, overwhelmed. Then, with a sigh, he began slowly scrolling through page after page, with the vague hope that something would strike a chord. 'Greenhill Management' was conspicuous by its absence, so he concentrated on looking through the results for the single word 'greenhill' which seemed to be predominantly houses of various types.

For each entry, he looked closely at the image displayed on the screen, still hoping that something might jog his memory and might seem familiar. He knew it was only a slight chance; 'greenhill' might have nothing to do with buildings. There were just too many results to look at. While looking, he resolved to give it up for now, and go to the police and ask for the crime number the insurance company needed. Then he could go back and see if they could give him any contact details for 'Greenhill Management.'

The police were a little bit of a problem. Having deserted the scene of a triple killing, one of which he was responsible for, he wasn't sure of his status. Was he a fugitive or had Keith Blakeley sorted it out despite his disappearing act? He imagined Keith Blakeley would have been just a little annoyed that he'd not done as he'd been instructed, but his instincts had been screaming at him not to be picked up by Blakeley's team, or by the police, for that matter. The only problem was money. He needed that insurance payment even though it wouldn't now be as much as he'd been hoping. Cara Bingham's cash wouldn't last him long. He decided to ring for the crime number, instead of going in person. He made the call as short as possible, and was relieved to end the call with no awkward questions.

Back in the insurance office, the manager seemed relieved to see him return.

"You seemed rather upset when you rushed out earlier, Mr. Gregson, he said as Gregson passed over the crime number.

"I just came over very faint and dizzy," Gregson lied, not concerned as to whether or not it sounded unconvincing. The man on the other side of the desk nodded sympathetically as he typed in the details to his computer. He pressed the 'enter key' with a dramatic flourish.

"Very straight forward, Mr Gregson. Your claim should be dealt with in just a few days and the money transferred to your account. Is there anything else I can help you with?"

"Thank you," said Gregson, rising from his seat. "There is just one question, if you can answer it."

"Yes, Mr. Gregson?"

"Can you give me details of how I can get in touch with Greenhill Management?"

"Let me see a moment." There was more tapping on the keyboard. "Here it is." The other man paused. "Oh dear, it just seems to be a Post Office box number in Wiltshire. There's nothing else on the system, I'm afraid."

"Wiltshire?"

"Yes. Do you want the box number?"

"No, thank you." A Post Office box number was of no use to him. He certainly didn't want to write to them.

In the library later, he refined his internet search to 'Greenhill, Wiltshire.' It seemed a long shot, but might be worth a try. A few pages of results were produced and he stifled another sigh as he began looking through them, viewing images and reading whatever details might be available. He was only on his seventh result when he felt he'd struck lucky. Greenhill House on Greenhill Down in a small village called Monkton Dauntsey on Salisbury Plain. Originally the centre of a farm co-operative, it was now inside the Army-owned section of the Plain used as a training area. In the fairly detailed history of the house, there was nothing that caught his eye, no mention of 'Greenhill Management', but there was a picture, taken from the drive looking back towards the house. It was a view he'd seen before. He knew he'd seen it before, from the rear window of a car as he was driven away. His heart lurched a little as he printed out the

144

information and the picture and made the decision to go to Wiltshire.

CHAPTER TWENTY-THREE

"Well then, Colin, what have you got for me?" Keith Blakeley was sipping Earl Grey tea from a bone china cup, an affectation he'd picked up at university. The matching saucer was on the blotter of his desk. As far as he was concerned, Earl Grey deserved the respect of bone china and didn't taste right any other way. Colin Lennon on the other hand, was cradling a lukewarm mug of black coffee; he never seemed to manage to drink it hot during office hours; there were just too many interruptions, too many calls on his time.

"I've called in some long-standing favours, sir, but nothing I've got is in writing." He sounded slightly regretful. Government departments pride themselves on the paper trails they keep. "It would seem that all of the files and documents relating to what we're interested in have either disappeared or been destroyed."

What a coincidence," Blakeley said drily, hoping it sounded as sarcastic as it was meant to. "So all we've got is hearsay, then?" He was disappointed, but not really surprised.

"Oh no, sir. I'd put a lot of faith in the people I've talked to, and they do all seem to agree with each other." Blakeley knew better than to ask who those people might be. His deputy would almost certainly not tell him anyway, and it was probably better not to know. He still felt slightly guilty about having sent Lennon away the other day with a flea in his ear, when he'd been reading the files about Sonia Fox and the others. Much of that was to do with his awareness that, if he so wished, Colin Lennon would be able to make his life a misery, head of the department or not.

"Go on, then, Colin. What have you found out?"

"It starts with Sonia Fox and Cara Bingham, sir. It seems there is, or should I say was, some bad blood between them."

"They knew each other?"

"Knew of each other, sir, but there was more to it than that. Much more." Blakeley took a sip of his tea. His deputy glanced in his coffee mug, grimaced, and put it on the desk. "Cara Bingham was involved in a long term relationship with a very undesirable person, sir. A man named Anthony Rawlings, a real wheeler dealer and as unscrupulous as they come. They were a match made in hell, sir, and deserved each other. Rawlings came to our attention when he started negotiations with crime syndicates across the European Union, particularly in Eastern Europe. Romania was one of his favourite destinations. When Cara Bingham was out of the country, Sonia Fox was sent to deal with him."

"Sonia Fox?"

"Yes sir. It had been decided by those who make such decisions that he needed to be removed and Sonia Fox was given the job."

"So Sonia killed Cara Bingham's lover?"

"Yes sir. The rumours are that she slept with him as well."

"Oh God. So the Bingham woman, a highly skilled killer, was looking for revenge on Sonia Fox, also a highly trained killer, for shagging and killing her lover?"

"In a nutshell, sir. It just so happened that their paths crossed again over this Joseph Fox thing."

"She was working for the Chinese?"

"Yes, sir. As always, for the highest bidder," Lennon said.

"Well, that explains why Bingham wanted Sonia Fox dead, but where does Gregson fit into all this? Why did she involve him, Colin?"

"That's a bit more complicated, sir. It may have been that she was trying to throw Cara Bingham off her track."

"By involving an innocent man? I don't think so, Colin, and I don't think you do either, do you?" His deputy wouldn't commit himself.

"I'm not sure, sir," was all he would say and then he paused. "About the Greenhill Project, sir. I think we should move on to that."

"Is there a link, Colin?" Blakeley asked.

"I think there may be, sir," Lennon admitted. "Sonia Fox is certainly one link," he said. Blakeley nodded, noticing the suggestion that there might be others.

"So tell me about Greenhill."

"As I told you sir, it was a highly classified project, a radical development of treatments normally used for personality disorders." Blakeley looked puzzled.

"Radical?"

"And controversial, even in the department. Psychologists work on altering a person's moods and attitudes by trying to change the way they think and deal with what they term negative thoughts. Stress management, anger management and things like that are all based on that theory." Keith Blakeley nodded again. "Greenhill went further than that. A lot further." Lennon paused again, as if gathering his thoughts. "The idea was to completely change a personality, erase all memories, everything, and start again, building a new person, new way of thinking, new reactions, all from scratch. A blank piece of canvas, as it were."

"Frankenstein gone mad," muttered Blakeley. "It's a horrific idea." Lennon ignored him.

"They were going to use a mixture of medication, brainwashing techniques and whatever else seemed suitable to achieve what they wanted. Apparently, disorientation was a major part of it, because if it's used long enough, it can even make someone forget who they are. A whole new set of memories would then be imposed using a drip technique."

"Like I said, Frankenstein." This time, Lennon agreed with his boss.

"Yes sir. It was very controversial and was as highly classified as it was to keep the number of people who knew about it to a minimum."

"Did it ever get off the ground?" Blakeley asked. Lennon nodded, but before he could say anything, Blakeley continued. "Who on earth could they get to try this stuff on? The civil liberties people and the Press would have had a field day with it if it had ever got out." Lennon could only agree with his superior about that.

"It was set up in an old farmhouse on Army land in Wiltshire, sir. That's where it got its name from: Greenhill."

"There's one thing that puzzles me, Colin. Why was Sonia Fox, with the background and skills she had, involved in a project like this? Wasn't it outside her area of expertise?"

"She requested the job, sir."

"Why on earth would she do that?" Blakeley asked.

"Two reasons, but her main job was supposed to be to deal with problems resulting from the treatments." Blakeley understood immediately what his deputy meant.

"But did they actually have anyone that they tried these techniques on, Colin?"

"If the rumours are to be believed, sir, then yes they did. Just one subject, and then the project was closed down, although some people are convinced it's just in a hiatus."

"Still running?"

"Yes sir, monitoring results."

"Are you telling me it worked, Colin?"

"I don't know, sir. I couldn't find out any more in that area." There was once more that unmistakable feeling that Blakeley often had of Lennon keeping something from him, but this was the first time he'd had the nerve to question his deputy on the matter. He was direct and to the point.

"What aren't you telling me, Colin? This is no time to hold anything back. You know who the guinea pig was, don't you?"

"I believe so, sir, and I don't think you're going to like it. The subject's name was Martin Grant." There was a stunned silence from Blakeley.

"'Curious and curiouser,'" he finally quoted. "So what have you found out about him, or what is it you didn't tell me when I read his file? There wasn't much in it, to say the least, was there Colin? Certainly no grounds for him to be selected for a project like this. Didn't it say he failed to return from a fact finding mission somewhere?" He thought about what he'd just said. "I presume that means he was spying?"

"Sort of, sir. He was in the same department as Sonia Fox..." Blakeley's shoulders sagged a little. "In fact he was her boss....and her lover." Blakeley exploded.

"Her boss? What the hell happened, Colin? Do you know?" Know? Of course I know, thought Lennon. I was involved in this mess right up to my eyeballs, but I'm damned if I'm going to admit it.

"There were rumours, sir. Grant had been involved in too many kills and went soft. Remorse and regret are not useful emotions in that line of work. He began to question the morality of what he was doing."

"And?"

"Under normal procedures, he would have been removed, simply killed, but with the Greenhill Project available, it was suggested he might be a useful subject."

"Suggested? Didn't he volunteer?"

"No sir. He was...well, just taken from his flat one night." Blakeley was silent for some time, his mind working feverishly, making connections and joining dots, before reaching a decision. Sometimes there are questions that you don't want to know the answers to, but that have to be asked anyway, no matter the consequences.

"Colin, how do you know all this? And don't give me any bullshit about calling in favours or protecting sources." Seeing a blank imperturbable look appear on his deputy's face, he continued quickly. "No lies, no prevarication. Just tell me the truth and tell me now." There was a pause while Lennon considered his answer, broken again by Blakeley. "You were part of this godforsaken project weren't you, Colin? That's how you know all of this stuff, isn't it?" Lennon nodded, obviously still reluctant to speak. "Then tell me about it, Colin. Tell me everything."

CHAPTER TWENTY-FOUR

After three days sojourn in Peterborough, Gregson felt ready to move. He'd read what he'd printed a number of times and had done more research on Greenhill, actually managing to find a floor plan of the building as it had last been known before being enclosed in the Army training area. It had apparently been deserted for years, and although standing on their land, not used by the Army for anything. It was the only part of Monkton Dauntsey on Army property, being almost a mile away from the village proper and was out of bounds to casual visitors, despite its long history and fine Tudor architecture. If he wanted to see it, he would undoubtedly be trespassing on Ministry of Defence property. So be it. He'd grown more certain that this was the place he needed to see.

It was a trouble free trip down to Wiltshire from Peterborough and driving into Marlborough, almost at the end of his journey, he stopped in the wide High Street. After lunch and coffee, in what he could only think of as a quaint tea-shop, he bought himself a map of the area immediately around Monkton Dauntsey, an Ordnance Survey Explorer, the most detailed they produced.

The route to Monkton Dauntsey from Marlborough, already fixed in his mind, was across downs dotted with prehistoric antiquities, none of which interested him. There was a certainty, single-mindedness and self confidence in his actions and planning which surprised him when he allowed himself to think about it. Too much self-analysis is harmful he'd been told, presumably by a psychologist, but he couldn't really remember. He knew he felt a different person from the man who'd sat in a deserted crematorium and watched his wife's coffin make its way into a fiery oblivion.

He drove quickly and steadily along the main road from Marlborough to Devizes, initially following the Kennet valley and then after Silbury Hill, a man made inverted cone with its top missing, which intrigued him for as long as it was in his line of sight, cutting across the downs. It was a good road, but he didn't want to draw attention to himself from any traffic police. He could still be a fugitive for all he knew. After Devizes, and a quick flash of panic at having to drive past the Police Headquarters, came the strangely named village of Potterne, and then it was out onto the predominantly Army-owned Salisbury Plain, with its tank crossings, occasional camps and numerous Ministry of Defence signs. When Monkton Dauntsey came into sight, the spire of its church elegant above the tree-line, he pulled off the road into a lay-by, turned off the engine and referred to his map. The main Devizes to Salisbury road, which he was on, cut through the middle of the village about a mile ahead of him; Greenhill was itself about a mile to the south of the village. As it was still only mid-afternoon, he decided on some sleep. What he had in mind for Greenhill was suited to semi-darkness. He put his seat back, set an alarm and hoped for sleep.

155

He slept soundly, despite the heavy traffic passing closely by. For the last few nights, even though the hotel bed had been extremely comfortable, he'd had numerous dreams disturbing his sleep. They'd vacillated unpredictably and erratically between the bloody scenes in the bed and breakfast and alarming images of the white room he didn't recognise, but which scared him all the same. What was that place, and why was he always dreaming about it, dreams that always seemed on the verge of turning into nightmares but never quite slipped that far? Whichever of the dreams it was, and it was quite often both, he was always left sweating and shaking.

The alarm he'd set up on his phone woke him and he was instantly alert, another new habit he'd developed recently. It was nearing dusk, with still just enough light to see, and time to move. He reached backwards into the back seat and grabbed hold of a small backpack which he pulled into the front. It contained some items he'd thrown together in Peterborough, most, admittedly, from what he'd found in Cara Bingham's car. The gun he'd taken from the bed and breakfast was in there, and it was the first thing he took out, placing it on the passenger seat next to him. A heavy duty screwdriver, a small lightweight torch, a knife, a bottle of water and a small first-aid kit made up the remainder of the contents, apart from two syringes, both filled with some sort of liquid, their needles protected by safety covers. Thankfully, there were labels on them, so he'd been able to find out what he was dealing with: Propofol, a powerful and dangerous anaesthetic. He remembered DI Townshend telling him it was what had been used to kill Tara Colman and Joseph Fox. One of the hypodermics was slipped back into the backpack and the other into his jacket pocket.

He turned on the map light on the car's dashboard to give him a clearer view of the OS Explorer and checked out on the map the landscape surrounding him. He found the house easily, and satisfied himself that it would be just as easy to find it on the ground. There was a lane leading to it from the centre of the village he could join by using a footpath from where he was. It should only be about fifteen to twenty minutes from where he was sitting. But could it be as easy as that? He hadn't forgotten it was on Army land. Getting out of the car, he leaned back in to get the pistol, which he tucked into the waistband of his trousers, and then leaned in again to grab the backpack, which he hooked over his shoulder. Locking the car, he crossed the road, climbed over a stile, and dropped down onto a slightly overgrown footpath.

CHAPTER TWENTY-FIVE

Sonia Fox had felt nothing but relief about Cara Bingham's death. Dramatic as it sounded, she'd known a showdown would come about between them at some time or another, but she'd wanted it on her own terms, and at a time and place of her choosing. Her brother's stupidity and Cara Bingham's involvement with the Chinese had put paid to those plans. Why on earth Joseph had ever thought he could pull one of his stunts on the Chinese government she couldn't understand and would now never know. She'd protected him often enough over his misdemeanours, pulled strings and kept him out of as much trouble as she could, but this time he'd paid the price for his greed and there had been nothing she could do about it. Apart from revenge. It was somehow satisfying that Cara Bingham wanted revenge on her for Tony Rawlings – God, but he'd been good in bed – but that she'd got in first for her little brother. Very satisfying.

She wasn't a woman prone to any form of regret or conscience, and never had been, except for the one love of her life, which had been taken away, but she did have one pang of sorrow over this whole affair with Joseph. Not him, nor the McNallys, although she had known them. Not the death of Cara Bingham, in her line of work that had simply been something waiting to happen, because that's what faced them all, nor the death of the unfortunate girl in Peterborough, whoever she may have been. No, it was for involving Malcolm Gregson, for lying to him, manipulating him, prising him out of his innocent world and then callously using him to achieve her own ends.

Slamming her foot to the floor on the accelerator of her eight cylinder BMW 650i convertible, she swept past an articulated lorry. A friendly toot on the horn and a cheery wave from the lorry driver in appreciation of being overtaken by a glamorous blonde in a fast car brought a smile to her face. With the top down, and the wind rushing past, she felt good. She always did, driving fast. She had just one problem left to sort out, and that was, unfortunately, Malcolm Gregson. She couldn't take the chance that he might become fully aware of what was going on, although that was the gamble she'd taken when she'd made her plans. She was also slightly concerned about the possible repercussions if he worked out her involvement in everything.

It wasn't hard for her to work out where he was going, because it was exactly where she wanted him. She'd been watching his movements, monitoring how things were developing and she knew how his mind worked, knew his thought processes. She'd also given him enough hints to point him in the right direction. What troubled her was whether or not she would be able to carry through what she knew needed to be done to tidy everything up. So far, he'd done very well, and everything had gone according to plan. After all it was because she knew him so well that she'd managed to get the task of looking after him, despite the reservations that some people had when she volunteered. Colin Lennon, although she didn't like the man, had been helpful then, but looking back she did think there might have been an element of malice in his assistance. He'd never liked the fact that they'd been so close.

Her concentration slipping as her mind worked on other thoughts, she rounded a bend too fast and found a slow moving tractor hauling a trailer right in front of her, just a little too close for comfort. A squeal of tyres caused by a touch on the brakes to avoid driving into the back of it, then another burst of speed to swerve past the vehicle and trailer, the BMW responding and handling beautifully. She completed her manoeuvre with a one finger gesture and a mischievous smile at a driver heading the other way who blasted his horn at her for her impudence.

She returned her thoughts to Colin Lennon, the smile turning almost malicious. Maybe she should engineer an encounter between Lennon and Malcolm Gregson, after having first given Gregson the right hints and subliminal instructions. She'd learned a lot from the Greenhill Project. Then, after providing Lennon with his just desserts, would be the time to deal with Malcolm himself. She shook her head and dismissed the idea, attractive as it was.

She passed the sign for Monkton Dauntsey and the car in the lay-by partly obscuring it without really noticing, entering the village that had become so familiar to her almost on autopilot. What had it been, four, five years since she'd been here? Certainly not long enough in the life of a village like this for much to have changed. Opposite the duck-pond and the lovely old church, she turned off into the lane leading to Greenhill. A large sign informed her that it was a no-through road leading to Ministry of Defence property, but there were no physical barriers preventing entry, just the polite signs. How well-behaved us English are presumed to be, she thought to herself.

Pulling up just through the gateway, the wooden gate now rotting and hanging forlornly from its hinges, she thought how little the house had changed, and how timeless it looked, just like the village. But unlike the very-much lived in village, Greenhill looked deserted and unwanted. It might have been her knowledge of what had gone on there, but she shivered in spite of herself. She'd never really liked the place, not from her very first visit and nothing that had happened since had changed her feelings. The area in front of the house, formerly a muddy mess of a farmyard, had been spread with gravel when the project moved in and it scrunched under the wheels of the BMW as she moved slowly forwards. She crossed to the track leading around the side of the building to the old barn, and parked the car in the same place she'd always parked it, cursing herself for being a creature of habit.

CHAPTER TWENTY-SIX

Gregson emerged from the footpath onto the lane leading to Greenhill surprised that there had been nothing to stop his progress onto Army property, as long as you discounted the overgrown brambles that had kept pulling at his clothes. The lane was much easier going, and then it was in front of him, 'Greenhill'. The sign, fixed on a wall by a rotting gate, was partially obscured by some climbing plant he recognised but couldn't name. He pulled it to one side and stood looking for a few moments. It chilled him for some reason, but not as much as the view of the house did when he straightened up and walked through the gateway. In the dim grey light of dusk, it looked almost menacing, roof and chimney stacks silhouetted against the sky. Without stopping, he walked across the forecourt, wincing with each step as his shoes noisily ground the gravel underfoot, disturbing the silence. There was still light enough to see that the weeds were taking over and that the door and windows were boarded up, but he didn't notice the recent tyre tracks in the gravel. He was more occupied with wondering how he was going to get inside the house.

Stepping up to the door, he tested the boarding to see how secure it was, frustratingly finding it very well done, and tastefully decorated with a sign saying 'MoD Property. Keep Out.' He started on a circuit of the building, checking each window and door he passed, approximately aware of where he was from his memory of the plan. He became increasingly more frustrated with each boarded up opening he checked and felt a growing edginess.

Finally, he was rewarded for his patience. A window, low to the ground, and near a set of French doors, had a loose board. Wishing it was the other way around and that it was the French doors with a loose board, he set to work with the large screwdriver, trying to prise it away from its fittings. Despite the apparently deserted and empty appearance of the building, he wasn't prepared to take any chances with noise, so worked as quietly as possible. When he finally got the board free, it gave him more space to work on the others covering the window, but it still took him almost forty five minutes to get enough room to climb through. Thankfully, the glass had already been removed, presumably when the place was boarded up.

Exchanging the screwdriver for the flashlight, he switched it on and shone the beam through the window and around the room. The last thing he wanted to do was climb in and find himself standing in a room behind a locked door. He saw a large room with two open doors leading into a passage of some sort beyond. Remembering the floor plan he'd studied, it was the dining room. He climbed in, swinging the beam down, just to ensure he wasn't lowering himself into a hole in the floor. Inside, the air was musty and stale, the floor thick with dust and massive cobwebs hung from the light fittings and from every corner of the room. As he walked, he noticed a trail of footsteps behind him on the floor and smiled to himself. There was certainly no way of disguising his entry and his presence.

Methodically, he searched room after deserted room, each recognisable from the floor plan in his head but from nothing else. He didn't know what he was looking for, only knew he was looking for something. He just hoped that if and when he found it, he would recognise it as the object of his search. Nothing caught his attention in any of the ground floor rooms. The house had been stripped of everything except those items described by estate agents as fixtures and fittings, and these, without exception, were empty, as were the walk-in pantries in the large kitchen. In each room it was the same story: dust and cobwebs.

The rather grand staircase looked solid enough from the bottom, but he tested each step carefully to check it was firm and would bear his weight before moving slowly upwards. The banister rail he ignored completely, staying close to the wall. Just in case. The upstairs rooms proved to be a repeat performance of downstairs, nothing to be seen but the detritus of desertion. A narrow stairway ran up to a small number of attic rooms, possibly servants' quarters, but these were again a disappointment. He went slowly down both flights of stairs and sat on the bottom step to think, reviewing the floor plan in his mind, carefully examining the image he held of each room until realisation hit him. A house this size and age would have been built with a cellar, so why hadn't he seen anything that looked like a cellar door? It should have been in the kitchen, but he hadn't noticed it. He rose and went back into what was once the kitchen, checking over the walls in the beam of his torch. There was nothing to be seen, but there should have been. He began tapping around the walls. Could the entrance to a cellar have been boarded up? When he discovered a hollow sound in response to his tapping, he thought the answer could well be yes.

He retrieved the screwdriver from his backpack and carried on tapping until he found what seemed to be the edge of the entrance and then used it to trace the outline, scratching plaster away. Holding the torch in his mouth while working proved tiring, so he had to keep stopping. How did they manage to do that in the movies? Eventually, he had the shape of a doorway outlined on the wall and had added quite considerably to the dust on the floor. Hoping the board used here was thinner than that used on the windows, he aimed a hefty kick at where he thought the centre might be. Thankfully it splintered slightly under the impact of his boot, so he followed that initial kick with others, until he had a hole large enough to give him leverage on pulling it apart. It proved easier than he thought it was going to be. Behind, he found a passage and steps leading downwards, so there was only one thing to do: he went down.

At the bottom of the flight of stone steps was a security door, looking completely out of place. He passed the now fading beam of the flashlight over it. There was no visible lock or keypad, just a handle, and hoping that luck would be on his side, he grasped it firmly and turned. The door opened silently and as it did so, lights began bursting into life along the corridor that was revealed behind. The sudden light almost blinded him and he blinked rapidly to adjust his eyes and dropped to a crouch, reaching for the gun he'd tucked into his trousers. The torch fell clattering to the floor. Prepared for anything, he was almost disappointed when nothing happened.

The corridor seemed to extend much further than the size of the building above and was lined with doors on each side. He checked each one out in the same way as he'd checked those upstairs, but this time with a gun in his hand instead of a torch. Each one he looked in seemed to be fitted out as an office, containing only empty shelves and grey metal standard government issue office desks. All other contents had been removed and none of them gave any indication of any other purpose they may have been used for. They were all painted in relaxing gentle pastel colours, a different one for each room.

Then a room stopped him in his tracks and set his mind whirling as soon as he opened the door. It was larger than the others, much larger, but like them painted in a pastel colour. There was a high ceiling and a metal table bolted to the middle of the floor, with plenty of space to walk around. Above this a light fitting was still hanging from the ceiling, the same type as those used in operating theatres. It made him shake. He'd seen that room before, from a prone position, the lights so bright they'd felt like they were burning his eyes. No matter how hard he tried, he'd not been able to close his eyes against the brightness, as if his eyelids had somehow been sewn open. He backed out into the corridor, pulling the door closed behind him.

Only one door then remained and standing by it, still not quite recovered from the operating theatre – it was the only way he could think of it – he was reluctant to enter, pausing with his hand on the door handle. He had the unsettling feeling that whatever was to be found behind that door was going to be unpleasant.

He opened it anyway; there was no point in running away now that he was here. Looking inside he almost sank to his knees, grabbing hold of the door frame, the gun falling from his hand. The room was white, unrelenting, unrelieved white; floor, ceiling, walls, all white. The only furniture was a white metal framed bed, again bolted to the floor. He staggered across to it and sat down, leaving his weapon where it had fallen. A tidal wave of despair and anger hit him and he sat immobile, staring at the wall, feeling himself slipping away, unable to stop himself edging towards a dark frightening mental pit. A voice brought him back to his senses.

"I knew you'd come," Sonia Fox said quietly from the doorway, but the uncertainty in her voice seemed to say otherwise, undermining her words.

CHAPTER TWENTY-SEVEN

"Hello, Malcolm," she said, when he didn't acknowledge her.

"That's not my name," he replied, looking round at her, his irritation plain "and you know it." His mind might suddenly be all over the place, but he was sure of that.

"Of course." She smiled. "I just thought you might be more comfortable with Malcolm." He nodded.

"Mmm, let's just stick with Malcolm, then, shall we?" he agreed. He wasn't really in the mood to argue anyway. It was her turn to nod.

"I owe you an explanation, don't I?" she said after a pause, sitting on the bed frame next to him. He noticed she was holding the gun he'd dropped.

"And an apology, I think."

"I've never done apologies, Malcolm. They don't change anything."

"It's never too late to start," he said, "but an explanation will do." He looked around the room and then gestured with his hand. "What's this all about, Sonia?" It seemed comfortable, using her first name, "and what's it got to do with me?"

"Do you remember anything about what went on here? You were here a long time, Malcolm."

"Strange dreams about this room, and a feeling that it was bad."

"It saved your life, Martin." He looked up sharply at her use of the name.

"What? How?"

"I said it saved your life. If you hadn't come here, you'd be dead." He looked puzzled. "We were lovers, Martin. You were my boss, and I wanted to save your life." He was getting used to Martin. It sounded right.

"Lovers?" He sounded surprised and wondered what it would be like to be the lover of this gorgeous woman.

"I couldn't let them kill you, Martin. And then when they wanted me to do it..." She felt she wasn't explaining this very well. It all sounded so jumbled, so disjointed. He put up his hand to stop her.

"Can we start with meeting again?" he asked. "We didn't know each other at school, did we?" She shook her head.

"No."

"So where did I get the idea that I had a crush on you and got tongue tied whenever I saw you?" She smiled, but he didn't give her a chance to answer. "You weren't married to Joseph Fox either, were you? Or trying to escape from the marriage?"

"No. Joseph Fox was my brother."

"So why all the lies?"

"Some of them were new memories, but yes, others were lies."

"But you knew me, yes? And you said we were lovers and worked together?" She nodded her head, but couldn't meet his gaze. There was anger in his voice now. "So tell me, Sonia, tell me why I can't remember a damned thing about it!" He hadn't intended his voice to become so loud, but there was no taking it back.

"We worked together, and you were in charge of the department. I fell for you..." He still couldn't imagine this beautiful woman having any feelings for him. He interrupted.

"Worked together? Doing what?"

"We both worked for the government," she said, then paused. "I'm not going to beat around the bush, Martin. We were trained to kill people and we were both bloody good at our jobs." That statement left him speechless, but made sense of the dreams he'd been having. On impulse he mentioned them.

"They were memories, not dreams," she explained.

"Memories that a man shouldn't have to carry around," he said quietly. Then he added "So what happened, Sonia?" It was her turn to look puzzled.

"Happened? What do you mean?"

"This place. Us. The snatches of memory I keep getting. My name. My life. All of it. What happened?"

"You went soft," she said flatly. "Remorse, regret, qualms of conscience, all of the stuff we're supposed not to feel, that's supposed to be trained out of us. And you wanted out."

"Out?"

"You got it into your head that because you were so well thought of, and head of a department, you'd be allowed to walk away, but that wasn't ever going to happen." As she spoke, he remembered his reaction after he'd killed Cara Bingham, and began to piece together what it must have been like, but was it invention or memory?

"And that's where this place comes in?"

"Yes."

"How?"

"It was a new project, and they named it after this place: the Greenhill Project." She was watching him for any reaction. He recognised it as a word she'd used in her contacts with him, but nothing else, and said so. She took his hand in hers. What he didn't tell her was that memories were coming back in dribs and drabs, and had been since the first mention of the word to him, in the foyer of the hotel in Peterborough. Had that been her intention all along, to unlock his memories? Her touch was something else, though, almost like an electric shock to his

171

system. Lovers. She'd said they'd been lovers. Her hand felt so soft against his and his mind willingly gave up some of its secrets. The touch of her skin as he gently stroked it with his fingers, the curve of her breasts under his hands, the sweet taste of her lips against his. He looked into her eyes, the desire he'd felt for her reviving. The love was still there on her face. She squeezed his hand.

"I've been looking out for you, Martin."

"Looking out for me?" He was confused, but the feel of her hand, the pressure she was putting on his, was very pleasant.

"Yes, because of the project." He felt she was skirting around the main point, but became distracted again as her fingers began caressing the back of his hand.

"What was the project, Sonia, and how did I end up here?"

"They were going to kill you when you went soft, and I was the person ordered to do it."

"You? Why?"

"I was next in seniority to you, and there was opposition to our relationship, mainly from a high-up prick named Colin Lennon. It was him who ordered your elimination, and him who I had to beg to get you on to the project instead." She hesitated when she remembered the things Lennon had made her do to get what she wanted.

"Did I know him? The name seems familiar."

"You hated each other."

"Oh.' There was a pause. "You still haven't told me what the project was all about, Sonia," he prompted.

"Greenhill was the only way to keep you alive. I couldn't bear the thought of you being dead, let alone being the one who killed you, Martin. It was better to know you were alive, even though I would have lost you anyway." She was rambling, and it took him a few minutes to digest what she was saying.

"So what happened here?" he gestured around the room. She surprised him by laughing, albeit bitterly.

"Well, if you can't remember anything, at least the project worked. People didn't think it would." The laugh turned into a sad smile.

"Oh, I'm remembering bits, but only since I saw you again. This room for instance, and that room along the corridor that looked like an operating theatre."

"So the trigger worked as well. The word 'greenhill' was planted in your mind as a memory trigger. That was another doubtful area."

"Sonia, tell me what this project did to me."

"The idea behind the project was to look into changing personalities and to go deeper into completely changing a person so that they would remember nothing of their former life. It used drugs, brainwashing, and torture techniques, anything that could conceivably change a person. That's where you came in."

"I volunteered?"

"No, Martin, far from it." There was so much sadness in her voice. "I suggested you to Colin Lennon as a subject. He took a lot of persuading. I'm sorry, Martin, so sorry, but I just couldn't see you dead." She paused again.

"Greenhill took my life away?"

"But left you alive," she insisted.

"Not really," he said. "Were you involved in what was done to me?"

"No," she said firmly, then changed her mind. "Yes, but only slightly. Obviously Colin Lennon knew about us, so he used me to check your memory, to see if you remembered me. The day you didn't, showed no signs of knowing who I was, was the worst day of my life. You were alive, but I'd lost you." She squeezed his hand again.

"And I became Malcolm Gregson, here in this god-awful room?" How could she have been party to this abomination? And she said she loved him? He pulled away from her slightly, releasing his hand from hers and felt something in his jacket pocket poke his side. He put his hand in and found the syringe he'd placed there earlier.

"Yes. When it was realised the treatment had worked, it was decided to try the proposed second stage of the project."

"There was more?"

"You were returned to a normal, mundane life, continuing the medication, of course. Everything was set up for you."

"Amanda?" Had his ex-wife been that or just another operative? Sonia shook her head.

"No, you weren't married."

"She was my keeper?" He was finding it harder and harder to believe what she telling him.

"Someone had to make sure you kept taking the medication, Martin."

"But I haven't had any since she died."

"No, and that helped with the return of memories."

"Where did you fit in on this second stage?" he asked.

"I volunteered to watch over you. It was the least I could do." She sounded sincere.

"And yet you brought me back, like bloody Lazarus, and took my life away a second time. Didn't you care at all?" She looked shocked. "Why did you bring me back, Sonia?" It was the question she'd been dreading.

"I needed you and there was no one else I could trust. I hoped that with what had been done here at Greenhill, I'd be able to

175

revive some memories, enough for you to help. I'd found out Cara Bingham was on my tail again and the only way I could deal with her was confuse her and take her by surprise."

"You should have killed the woman when you dealt with Rawlings," he said, startled by remembering. She was equally surprised.

"You remembered that?" she said.

"It just came out of nowhere," he admitted, but didn't add that the memories were trickling back faster and faster as they talked.

"The department didn't want her dead, Martin. She was too useful. If you remember, it was your decision."

"You wanted me to kill her for you," he said abruptly.

"Yes." Her voice sounded small. "I was out of practice after the time spent here at Greenhill and watching over you. I didn't know if I could take her, Martin."

"And you thought I could? After everything I'd ever been taught had been suppressed in some black hole of my mind?" He was finding it hard to control his temper. "That I could kill a killer, when I'd been turned into a meek and mild council clerk? What were you thinking?"

"I hoped..."

"Hoped? That's a bloody joke. I was expendable, wasn't I, Sonia? It wouldn't have mattered if I hadn't done what you wanted, because I'd be dead and out of the way, wouldn't I?"

"But you did kill her, Martin, didn't you?"

"Yes I did, and I felt the same way as I had done before. Think about that, Sonia. You said it yourself: I'd gone soft, and yet knowing that you still got me to kill for you. What sort of hard hearted bitch would do that to someone she says she loved?" She'd expected the anger and it had been longer coming than she'd thought, but the degree of his anger surprised her. She took his hand again and moved closer to him until her breast was brushing his arm. Desire might still turn him her way. "You used me, Sonia. For your own ends, you used me. To save your own skin." His voice was flat. She tried to snuggle closer. The coldness in his voice made her shiver. "You say I loved you once, but I can't see how. You're a cold and dangerous bitch, Sonia Fox." She gasped as she felt a sharp stabbing pain just above her kidneys, but was dead before he'd even finished emptying the syringe into her.

CHAPTER TWENTY-EIGHT

With Sonia slumped in his arms, he remembered. Everything. In a flood, it all came back, everything he'd done, everything he'd been, but especially her. He remembered how good it was to feel her in his arms, to fall asleep holding her close and to wake still cuddling her. He remembered the feel of her body as they made love, their bodies entwined in a rising rhythm of passion. He remembered, and as he did so, tears began to roll down his cheeks, and he kissed her hair.

With the remembering came understanding. Would he have done anything different if the tables had been turned? Probably not. They were who they were. He'd called her cold and dangerous, but the description was just as apt for him as her, for Cara Bingham and for anyone in their line of work. They wouldn't be capable of doing it if they weren't. The only difference was that he'd realised and been foolish enough to think he could walk away. He kissed her hair again, knowing despite what he'd said to her, that he did love her once.

"How sweet, the two star-crossed lovers in each other's arms for one last time." He knew the voice, knew it and disliked its owner. He didn't look up, just wondered idly why Colin Lennon was here at this moment, a moment he needed to himself. The man was intruding, sticking his nose in where it wasn't wanted, something he'd always been good at. Grant's sorrow began to change, to mutate into something far more dangerous, and he laid Sonia's body carefully and reverently on the bed frame. Then he allowed himself to explode into anger, a raging anger that was directed solely at Colin Lennon.

The man might have been holding a gun, and might even have been prepared to use it, as Martin Grant, for that was who he was now, through and through, launched himself from the bed. Lennon didn't stand a chance, didn't get the opportunity to use his weapon, or even to land a blow. A diving head-butt to the stomach took him to his knees, knocking the gun from his grasp. He was still gasping for breath as Grant was quickly up on to his feet, swinging a vicious kick to Lennon's jaw, laying him out flat on the floor, only just conscious enough to register a very angry man standing over him.

"You bastard, Lennon. You should have had me killed when you had the chance, not stuck me in this hell." There was no confusion now in Martin Grant's mind between Malcolm Gregson and himself. This was Martin Grant speaking, the voice of a killer. It was the last voice and the last words Colin Lennon ever heard. The fear in his eyes disappeared along with his life as Grant aimed a sharp straight fingered jab to his throat, delivered with all the force and anger he could muster, and crushed his windpipe.

Grant felt exhausted. Two more killings he was responsible for. Two more lives extinguished. He returned to his seat on the bed frame, one hand resting on Sonia's hip. With the other hand, he pulled his mobile out from his jacket.

"It's over, Blakeley," he said without preamble, when the connection was made.

"Over, Malcolm? What's over?" Blakeley asked innocently.

"That's not my name," Grant replied wearily.

"No, it's not, is it Mr. Grant." If Keith Blakeley was surprised at who was ringing him, he didn't sound it. "I take it you're ringing in a successful job?"

"In a way. More like confessing to a double murder."

"Miss Fox?"

"Dead." A dullness had entered Grant's tone and didn't go unnoticed by Blakeley in his London Office.

"Probably for the best, she had become a little unreliable. Lennon?"

"Dead." Again the dull, flat tone, Blakeley noticed.

"Mmm. I didn't think he would stand much of a chance against either you or Miss Fox."

"You sent him?" Grant asked.

"Yes. He wouldn't have come of his own accord, Mr. Grant, and someone had to tidy up for the department. He seemed the ideal choice." If Grant wasn't very much mistaken, Keith Blakeley sounded rather pleased at the outcome of his instructions for Colin Lennon, and Blakeley did indeed have a self-satisfied smile on his face.

"Now what happens?" asked Grant.

"Walk away, Mr. Grant. You won't be bothered again in any way, so take the opportunity to get on with your life. Walk away and forget." The phone went dead. Grant took one disgusted look at it in his hand and threw it on the floor, grinding it to pieces under the heel of his boot.

Forget? Walk away? How could he possibly do that? He remembered everything, every assignment, every kill. He wasn't going to be able to forget, nor did he think he'd be able to live with the knowledge of all that he'd done. Absently, he stroked Sonia's hair and cheek and kissed the tip of her nose. Then he stood up again, grim-faced. Stepping over Lennon's inert body, he left the room and walked up the full length of the corridor, back to where he'd dropped his torch and backpack. Leaving the flashlight where it was, he picked up the backpack and walked slowly back to the room, his expression now set and determined. Sitting once more on the bed frame, he glanced down at Sonia as he opened the flap on the backpack, reaching inside to pull out the second of Cara Bingham's deadly syringes of Propofol. As he sat staring off into space, twiddling the syringe in his fingers, the tears started to come again.

EPILOGUE

In the misty early hours of the morning, with most sensible people still in their beds, there was no one but two weary attendants at the crematorium to witness the arrival of a filthy white Transit van, its number plates all but invisible under the dirt and mud accumulated during its travels. As it parked in the loading bay, they almost nonchalantly removed its small load of body bags and unceremoniously and untidily dumped them onto an old trolley. The driver of the van remained in his cab, not getting out even to exchange a few words with them, and was pulling away into the night almost before one of the attendants could get the rear doors shut again. The two men watched as the van sped off, and then turned to their delivery.

Alerted by a phone call and a keyword that had jerked them wide awake, the two men had been coming to the end of a busy night of feeding the furnaces, the grisly but vital backroom job of a crematorium, and were now stifling yawns as they pulled the trolley back towards the building, a squeaking wheel the only sound accompanying the bodies on their final journey.

Note from the author:

Thank you for reading this book.

I hope you enjoyed reading it as much I enjoyed writing it.

Contact me at:

Beckybooks2014@gmail.com

Or on Facebook:

www.facebook.com/pages/Beckybooks/1410 873395829447

Or read my blog:

http://beckybooks2014.wordpress.com

45045703R00105

Made in the USA
Charleston, SC
10 August 2015